In a panic, I went down on my knees in front of the black iron stove, my hands trembling. I opened the little door. Inside, the grate was indeed heaped with a load of dead gray ashes. I looked around for something to clean it out with. The guard guessed what I was looking for.

"Use your hands, use your hands," he snarled. "What's the matter, afraid to get your hands dirty? That's where you belong, you little Jewish brat, wallowing in the dirt."

Blinking back tears, I began to sweep handfuls of ashes out of the grate. The ashes were still warm, but not hot enough to burn me. But he couldn't have known that, I thought in fury. He wanted me to get burned!

He was still standing over me, so close that I could feel his legs touching my back. Once I looked up and saw his eyes, steely gray eyes, staring at me in such an odd way, as if he were measuring me with them. I went back to my ashes, trying to control my trembling. He mustn't know how scared I am, I thought. I don't want him to have that pleasure.

MARIETTA D. MOSKIN is a writer of children's books who lives in New York City. The events in *I Am Rosemarie* are drawn from her own wartime experiences and from those of her relatives and friends. Mrs. Moskin came to live in the United States in 1946 after the end of World War II.

ALSO AVAILABLE IN LAUREL-LEAF BOOKS:

I AM ROSEMARIE

MARIETTA D. MOSKIN

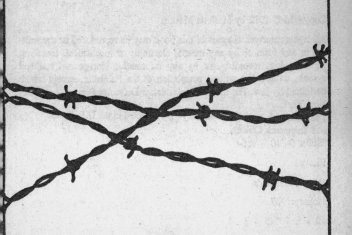

LAUREL-LEAF BOOKS

LAUREL-LEAF BOOKS bring together under a single imprint outstanding works of fiction and nonfiction particularly suitable for young adult readers, both in and out of the classroom. Charles F. Reasoner, Professor Emeritus of Children's Literature and Reading, New York University, is consultant to this series.

Published by
Dell Publishing
a division of
Bantam Doubleday Dell Publishing Group, Inc.
666 Fifth Avenue
New York, New York 10103

To my mother,
who taught me never to give up—
with love and gratitude

ISBN: 0-440-94066-4

RL: 6.3

Printed in Canada

January 1987

10 9 8 7 6 5 4 3

CONTENTS

Amsterdam

MAY 1940-August 1942

Chapter 1

I SHOULD HAVE SLEPT late on that bright May morning because spring vacation had started and I didn't have to get up to go to school. Instead I woke up at five fifteen — hours before my normal schedule. Half annoyed, half pleased with the knowledge that I didn't have to hurry, I closed my eyes again and prepared to go back to sleep.

But sleep wouldn't come. Through my half-open window the backyard noises of an awakening neighborhood intruded on my consciousness: the sharp clatter of a garbage can being closed, the thin wail of a baby, the strident cry of a tomcat early aprowl among the backyard fences.

And then, almost like a backdrop to those other, more familiar noises, there was a low but steady droning sound, punctuated now and then by an extended but muted rumbling. Like far-away thunder, I thought sleepily. But how could it be thunder on such a gloriously sunny day?

Lazily I let my mind drift back to other, more immediate matters. What, for example, would I do with my first vacation day? I'd spend it with Anneke most likely — Anneke, my best friend, who lived just across the backyards on the next street. Anneke would be the one who'd make the plans for us. She usually did and I was glad to let it be that way. Perhaps we'd take our bikes and ride out to the sandy dunes just beyond the edge of our South Amsterdam neighborhood. I had received a brand-new shiny bike for my twelfth birthday just a few days ago and I was eager to try it out on a longer ride.

I wondered whether Anneke too was lying awake in bed right now, listening to those strange rumbling and droning noises that seemed to grow louder and more insistent all the time. How irritating that I couldn't identify those sounds. Like airplanes, I thought, lots of them, droning high through the blue skies overhead. But why would a swarm of airplanes disturb the almost rural quiet of Amsterdam's southern district? It was a rare day when any airplanes passed over our house.

Suddenly I remembered: of course — the mo-bilization! People had talked about little else for weeks and weeks. Ever since Germany and En-gland had gone to war in the fall before, my parents and their friends had spent endless hours discussing Holland's chances of remaining neutral. Wedged in between the two warring nations, Holland was hard pressed to stay out of their fight. Finally, a few weeks ago, the government had reluctantly mobilized Dutch troops as a precautionary measure, deploying the army mostly along the German frontier.

The more I thought about it, the more I was sure that those odd rumbling sounds were made by guns stationed more than halfway across the country. But what an ungodly hour for war maneuvers! Of course, soldiers always had to get up very early, didn't they?

I made a mental note to ask Anneke about those war games when we met later on. Anneke's oldest brother had been called into the army a couple of weeks ago and she might know more about what those soldiers were doing near the German frontier.

Satisfied that I had figured out what had puzzled me, I dismissed the distant guns from my mind. And almost immediately I was distracted by different noises — closer and more demanding ones — right in the house.

There were footsteps in the hall and on the stairs, doors being opened and closed, hushed voices in front of my bedroom door. What in heaven's name were my parents doing up before six?

A possible answer came to me quickly: Grannie! That's what it probably was. Grannie — in the room right next to mine — having another one of her recurring heart attacks.

I jumped out of bed and ran out into the hall. There was no one about. The door to Grannie's room was open, but her room was empty. So was my parents' large front bedroom.

Buttoning my bathrobe over my pajamas, I ran down the stairs. Already halfway to the downstairs landing I could hear voices coming from the living room — my parents' voices and my grandmother's — and then the loud, urgent voice of a radio announcer.

"Parachutists," the voice kept saying. "Beware of parachutists. Stay off the streets. Do not trust strangers. Warning! Warning! Parachutists!"

The loud voice echoed through the downstairs hall, but I was in too much of a hurry to try to make sense of the words. I burst into the living room and then stopped short.

My parents and my grandmother were near the radio, listening so intently that they didn't even notice that I had come into the room until I called to them. Then my parents came over to me, their faces grave.

I looked from them to my grandmother, who was still hovering near the large, old-fashioned shortwave radio set.

"I heard all the noise — I thought it was Grannie," I said.

"We are at war, Rosemarie," my father said quietly — so quietly that at first I didn't grasp the meaning of his words.

"War?" I repeated stupidly. "But there is a war and we are neutral. We're not going to get into this war."

"You tell that to Hitler," Grannie said sharply behind my father's back. "We should have expected it — everybody should have expected it.

After Czechoslovakia and after Austria and Poland — it was stupid to think he would give a hang about neutrality."

"Germany invaded Holland without a warning during the night," my father explained.

War. Invasion. How often had I heard these words used in conversations during the past year or two without really listening to them. Wars and invasions happened to other people, but not to us — not to safe, neutral, and peaceful Holland. Even the words seemed unreal, spoken as they were in the familiar surroundings of our sunny living room.

Reality was my father, looking oddly impeccable in his patterned silk bathrobe even at this unaccustomed morning hour. And my mother . . .

For the first time since I had come into the room I really looked at my mother. Her face had been drained of all color and there were traces of tears around her eyes and on her cheeks. With my father's arm around her, she seemed strangely still and vulnerable. This was an unaccustomed mood for my mother, who had always seemed like a tower of strength to me. It was that unexpected look of terror on her face that made my own throat go dry.

"What will we do, Daddy?" I cried, clutching his arm. "What's going to happen now? Our soldiers are fighting the Germans, aren't they? Our army will win?"

My father drew me close to him with his free arm, the other one still around my mother.

"Nobody knows yet," he said. "Germany launched a massive paratrooper attack. No one has any idea how many German soldiers have been parachuted behind Dutch lines in civilian clothes. That's why they keep issuing these warnings over the radio. Anyone found in the streets speaking with a German accent is suspect."

"I guess I'd better stay indoors then," Grannie said with a wry smile.

Her attempt at humor seemed to break the tension, although it made us all realize that we had been talking in German — the language of what was now the enemy.

There were times when I hardly remembered that I had not been born in Holland. I had been very young when my parents had come here for business reasons from their native Austria. I had mastered the Dutch language quickly and perfectly — much better than my parents, who still could not pronounce some of the more difficult throaty sounds without clearly betraying their foreign origins. At home my parents preferred to speak their own soft Austrian German to each other and to me, but I didn't care because I had become so completely bilingual that I scarcely noticed which language was spoken at any particular time.

Grannie, of course, hardly spoke Dutch at all. She had come to Holland less than two years ago, after Grandpa had died in Vienna and after Hitler's troops had annexed and occupied Austria.

Even though I was only ten at that time, I still remembered how worried my parents had been about their many relatives in Vienna when the first news came of the German "Anschluss."

It all had something to do with being Jewish and with Hitler's unreasonable hatred of the Jews. I suppose that was really the first time that I had actually thought about being Jewish. Before that it had been just another facet of my existence — accumulated and accepted in that offhand way in which children learn most facts about themselves. My family had always been rather casual about religion. The subject rarely came up in my daily life.

During the year that followed, a constant stream of uncles and aunts and cousins arrived as refugees in our house — all of them bound for South America or the United States. They talked about Hitler's persecution of the Jews, about sudden arrests and tortures, about stolen property and confiscated homes. I listened wide-eyed to the gruesome stories, shivering at the fate of nameless strangers, rejoicing that my relatives had escaped the worst. But when, one by one, they left our home to start their long sea voyage to the New World, I was glad to put those problems out of my mind again. Once again Hitler's threat became vague and distant, something that affected other people somewhere far away.

And now suddenly the danger was here. I tried to picture those enemy planes high in the cloudless sky, disgorging squadrons of soldiers in disguise to descend on the unsuspecting Dutch people. There was something almost gay in the image of all those civilians floating down through the air suspended from billowing parachutes.

And the muffled, faraway sounds of the guns didn't really sound menacing either . . . more like festive fireworks.

But the menace of the situation was clearly reflected in the almost frozen faces of my parents and grandmother and in the urgent voice of the radio announcer. In spite of the warm sunshine pouring into the living room through the wide French windows, I felt a shiver run down my back.

"Perhaps we'd better have some breakfast," my mother said suddenly. These were the first words she'd said since I had come downstairs and it sounded odd hearing her say something so ordinary for she still looked pale and disheveled and was trembling a little.

I watched as she tied her pale blue robe and tucked in the straying wisps of bright blond hair. With these simple gestures she seemed to take command of the situation — to accept the challenge of the war and all it might bring to us.

"Come on, Rosie — give me a hand," she said to me as she started to walk toward the kitchen. "There is nothing like a good cup of hot tea to clear our minds."

It was a strange breakfast. We all pretended to eat, buttering the crisp rolls and stirring sugar into our teacups — but in the next room the radio was still calling warnings about spies and paratroopers and the salvos of gunfire suddenly didn't seem quite so far away.

I stared out of the dining room window at the quiet sunny street outside. The street was deserted, as it would be at this early hour in the morning, and it seemed strange to think that somewhere out there among the neat brick buildings, spies and enemies might be lurking, ready to pounce on unwary passersby.

After breakfast we all went to get dressed. And we had hardly assembled downstairs again when Mr. van Dam, the block warden, rang our doorbell.

"You've heard the news," he said sadly. "Now we must put our emergency procedures into operation. We want a total blackout for tonight."

My father nodded. "Of course. We'll take care of it. But tell me, Henk — what else can I do?"

Mr. van Dam hesitated. He looked at my father oddly. There was a strange, long silence which Mr. van Dam tried to cover by clearing his throat at length.

"I'm afraid, Charles . . . it would be best if you'd stay right here at home," he said at last, looking terribly uncomfortable. "Of course I know you're not sympathetic to the German cause . . . but feelings are mounting against anything German right now . . . people are apt to throw Germans and Austrians in one pot. You do understand it's nothing personal, Charles, don't you?"

Two bright red spots appeared on my father's cheeks. He is angry, I thought. He always looks like this when he is angry. But my father controlled himself. "I guess there is plenty for me to do right here," he said.

I ran out of the room so I wouldn't have to shake hands with Mr. van Dam when he left.

He hadn't said it, but he had implied that we were considered enemy aliens! How could anyone think that we were in sympathy with the Nazis when all our relatives had had to flee Austria and when we probably hated them more than anyone else around!

For the next few hours we were busy carrying out the emergency procedures so that none of us had much chance to worry about the war or about our own special situation. We filled the bathtub and some extra pails with water and we brought in buckets of sand from the empty lot on the corner. This was a precaution against fires. To safeguard ourselves against flying glass in case of a bombing attack, we cut newspapers into long strips and pasted them in a criss-cross pattern on all the windows. We worked like an assembly line. Grannie sat at the dining room table, cutting the strips. I smeared the strips with thick white paste made of cornstarch and water, while my parents took turns standing on the kitchen stepladder to fasten the strips to the windowpanes.

We stopped briefly for lunch and that brought us to the question of our food supplies.

"You can be sure hoarding will start right away," Grannie said. "It did in 1914. I remember it well. Like locusts they were — descending on all the stores and emptying the shelves. Maybe we'd do well to lay in a few supplies ourselves. Sugar and canned milk and soap. Those are the things you'd be likely to need."

"I'm more concerned about some groceries to tide us over the next few days," my mother said. "If we are really to be confined to our house, who is going to do the shopping for us?"

This led to a lively discussion whether it was safe for any of us to go to the stores under the circumstances. In the end my mother decided to send me.

"Nobody will ask a twelve-year-old whether she is a traitor," she declared. "Besides, Rosemarie speaks Dutch without an accent. She can take her bicycle and bring the groceries home in the basket."

I was glad to get out of the house. I wanted to get out, among other people, to be reassured it wasn't all as bad as it seemed at home.

But the mood in the grocery store was not reassuring. The counter was mobbed by excited women clamoring for everything from sugar to candles and lard.

I found the nice gray-haired clerk who knew me and he put a pound of sugar and two bars of soap in front of me before he even looked at my mother's list.

"One pound per customer," he told me. "You might as well get yours."

Back home I found my mother sitting in the living room, sewing two old bedspreads together to make into makeshift blackout curtains.

"I'm glad you're back, Rosemarie," she said. "There are so many rumors about. Mrs. Dijkman from next door dropped by and she told us that there are barricades up and street fights going on all over the country. Only Amsterdam seems to be quiet so far."

That night incendiary bombs fell on Amsterdam. The air-raid sirens screamed their warnings into the still darkness of the night, rousing us from our beds. We had heard the shrill sirens before — but then it had been only a test. This was the real thing.

Using the small beam of my flashlight, I found the clothes and small suitcase we had prepared for such an emergency before we went to bed. Downstairs I found the rest of the family assembled in the entrance hall.

"Should we go to the air-raid shelter?" my mother wondered. My father shook his head.

"I think we'd be just as well off in our own basement or right here, under the stairs. They say the safest place in a building is always under the stairs."

No doubt my father had learned all of this during his civil defense training when he had learned to be a fireman. At the time it had struck me very funny to imagine my staid, sedate father climbing fire ladders and handling long, snaking hoses. Now it didn't seem funny anymore. But I agreed with him about the air raid shelter. We had watched it being built on the empty corner lot, a simple structure made of beams and sandbags, the sloping sides and flat roof camouflaged with squares of sod to make it look like the rest of the grassy plot from the air. All the neighborhood children had played in and around that shelter for weeks — it had made a wonderful playhouse. But I couldn't believe that shelter would stand up under a bombing attack.

We sat on the floor in the narrow hall, under the stairs, waiting for the bombing to stop. Occasionally we heard distant explosions and the sharp ack-ack from the antiaircraft guns mounted on the roof of the high school just across the street.

Twice my father went to the front window to reconnoiter. He came back shaking his head.

"Those fools," he muttered. "They run out on the street to pick up bits of flack or spent shells from the antiaircraft guns. Don't they know they could get killed that way? Souvenir hunting in the middle of a bombing raid!"

"They aren't used to being in a war yet," my mother said. "People have to learn how to behave in a war — it doesn't come naturally."

The next wave of bombs seemed to fall a good deal closer. We could hear the whining sound of their descent before the loud detonations made the whole house tremble.

"They say as long as you can hear the bomb on its way down, it is far enough away not to fall on top of you," Grannie said gamely. "The dangerous ones are the ones you don't hear."

Still, it was an eerie sound. Four, five, six bombs fell in quick succession, each one seemingly closer than the last. Finally the all-clear signal released us from our cramped station under the stairs.

"Go back to bed, Rosemarie," my mother told me. "But keep your clothes on just in case."

My mother was right. Twice more that night the shrill sirens summoned us from our beds. Twice more we huddled in the darkness, waiting for the all-clear sound.

Somehow the whole war seemed like an endless period of waiting. We waited for the air raids to come and pass, we waited for news or even rumors, we waited for the British to come across the Channel in order to save Holland from the German attack. Nobody doubted that the British would come. It was just a question of time.

My family spent a good part of those war days sitting around the dining room table, because this room, with a window to the street, was our closest contact with the outside world.

"We should have left with the others," Grannie wailed for the fiftieth time, shaking her head. "We should have listened to the warnings."

There had been warnings, I remembered. When war first had broken out between Germany and England, our relatives had written to us from the United States, asking us to join them in the New World. Some of my parents' friends had left at that time too and they also had urged us to go with them. But my father had refused.

"I'm not going to run away," he had insisted. "We are settled here and we feel this is our home. That's why we are placing our bets with the future of this country."

I had felt proud of my father at such times. I loved Holland and I would have hated to leave my adopted country. Now it seemed that my father and I had been wrong.

"Maybe we still should leave," my mother said slowly. Her eyes traveled through the open window to the blue Ford sedan parked invitingly right in front of our door.

"But we are under curfew," my father reminded her. "How far do you think we'd get even if we started out? Don't you think they'd have roadblocks on the way to the shore?"

"Well, what about the risk of waiting here for a German occupation?"

My father didn't answer. It was a question that couldn't be answered. They had asked it a hundred times or more.

I couldn't stand to listen to the conversation any longer. Crossing the living room, I went out into the garden through the French doors.

I stared at the flagstones of the patio. Sometime, in the distant past of my childhood, I had scratched a hopscotch grid into the stones. Now I could see its faint outline reflected by the sun. Almost automatically I picked up a pebble and began to play. It was a childish thing to do, but I longed for movement, for action, and the familiar rhythm of the game was reassuring too.

Waiting for the Germans? Surely that wouldn't happen. It couldn't happen! The British would come. They had to come!

Two days later, the British still hadn't come. Instead, the Germans mounted a murderous bombing attack against Rotterdam — practically leveling that harbor city to the ground. The devastating news filtered slowly into Amsterdam the next morning, spreading a sense of doom and horror in its wake.

That evening we gathered around the radio to listen to a message from the Queen. In shocked silence we listened as Queen Wilhelmina haltingly bade farewell to her people. The Queen spoke to us from aboard a ship already on the high seas — bound for exile in England. She asked her people to be brave and patient and she promised to work unceasingly for our liberation from abroad.

The Queen's voice was familiar, but I simply couldn't grasp the meaning of her words. It couldn't be true — the Queen couldn't really have left us — she couldn't just leave her country alone!

But it was true. The royal family had left the palace in the dark of the night. The Queen wanted to keep some sort of Dutch government alive abroad, but I found it hard to accept her reasons. I felt betrayed, abandoned. The country was doomed. We all had tears in our eyes when the broadcast ended.

"Well, this is it," my father said quietly when it was over. "We might as well face it now — Holland has lost the war."

Sometime during that night what was left of the Dutch government surrendered. The war was over for us.

The next day we watched from behind closed windows as the German army goose-stepped cockily into Amsterdam. Only a few Nazi sympathizers cheered the soldiers as they marched into the country they had conquered through treachery.

"I have a strange feeling that this is where I came in," Grannie said, staring grimly down on the helmeted soldiers. "Two years ago I watched them march into Vienna like this. Only there a lot of people were cheering. Otherwise, it's just the same."

"It's not the same," my mother said harshly. "In Vienna the people who wanted to flee could flee. The world around Germany and Austria was open. But now we are at the end of the line. This is a trap. We're surrounded by war and by the sea and there is no place to go. It's not the same at all!"

"At Anneke's house they are not talking about fleeing," I said. "They are talking about forming a resistance movement — about helping to liberate Holland from within."

"It takes time to mount a resistance movement," my mother said. "Anneke and her family have time to wait — they aren't Jewish."

The words exploded like a time bomb in my memory. Jewish! All the snatches of conversation I'd overheard, all the horror tales I had listened to and forgotten, all the bits of information I had unwittingly collected over the years, now suddenly came together to make sense.

We're in a trap, my mother had said. I thought of the white rat Anneke's brother had kept as a pet. A big fat white rat in a small wire cage. It was not a pleasant picture.

Below our window the last of the jackbooted German soldiers marched past and disappeared from sight at the end of the street.

Chapter 2

I FOUND OUT soon enough what it was like to be Jewish in a country occupied by the Nazis. The identity cards came first. Everyone in Holland had to have one. But ours bore a big red "J" for Jew.

"Why don't the Germans like Jews?" I asked my mother when we first got the cards. My mother shrugged her shoulders.

"Anti-Semitism is nothing new," she said. "It's happened before — in different times and places. It's just that Hitler is so fanatical about his hatred. His special persecution of the Jews can't be explained."

It felt strange, being singled out like that among all my friends. In harsh red print the card proclaimed: This person is different — this person is a Jew!

Card in hand, I looked at myself in the bathroom mirror. Did I look different? Had I changed overnight? But my face looked back as it always had: brown braids, round face, hazel eyes.

"Can people tell I am Jewish just by looking at me?" I asked.

"No, darling — you don't look Jewish. But they'll know if they check your card."

Looking Jewish? I'd never thought about that. Did I know people who looked Jewish? Did people look Protestant or Catholic? How could you tell?

I studied my card again. Rosemarie Sarah Brenner, it said. I'd never had a middle name, but now I did. By decree of the Nazis: "All Jewish females are to bear the middle name Sarah. All Jewish men will add the middle name Isaac." Charles Isaac Brenner read my father's card.

I stared into the mirror.

"Rosemarie Brenner," I said. "I am Rosemarie Brenner."

I didn't want to be different. I didn't want to change. But already there was a change. It said so in cold print on my card. If they could change your name by decree you *were* different. Just as they had taken my Austrian citizenship. All Jews are stateless, the Germans declared.

Who was I? What was I? I wondered. I wasn't sure anymore.

Week by week there were other changes. Some affected everyone. The rations cards did, and the curfews. But some were for Jews alone. Some professions were closed to Jews, some areas in the country, some places like theaters and movie houses.

The weeks lengthened into months.

My father lost his job too. The Austrian firm that had sent him to Holland wouldn't have Jews on their staff now. My father went into a kind of partnership with one of his non-Jewish friends afterwards, but he spent little time at his new office. Most of his time and effort were spent in the anterooms of various neutral embassies. Maybe one of them would give us visas — maybe we might be able to get away from Holland after all. There was Cuba . . . and the Dominican Republic . . . there even was Portugal. . . .

It was odd, finding my father home so often in the middle of the day now. But then, a lot of things were odd. Just walking around Amsterdam was different. The streets were as crowded with bicycles as ever, but automobile traffic was dominated by military vehicles. Ordinary drivers found it impossible to get gasoline. On the sidewalks, the uniforms of the various German occupation troops were much in evidence. Civilians stepped aside to let the conquerors pass, their eyes hard and their mouths compressed in silent anger. Most people had to be content to let their eyes betray their feelings. Too many sudden arrests had followed incautiously spoken words. But the hardest stares were reserved for the black-clad members of the Dutch security police. They were the traitors who were collaborating with the Germans in the humiliation of their own people.

Dutch people who betrayed their own! You had to see it to believe. No wonder the people had changed. They were somber and drawn into themselves, suspicious often even of old friends and neighbors. There was little gaiety and joy, and laughter generally was reserved for bitter jokes about our sad condition.

We had lived less than a year with the occupation, but already it seemed forever. I walked around, with my special identity card burning a hole in my pocket. What if people could tell, regardless of what my mother had said?

Down the street came martial music and the sound of marching feet. I craned my neck. A group of NSB girls came down the middle of the road, forcing traffic to the sides. They were the Dutch collaborationist version of the German Hitler Youth, smart in their blue uniforms as they marched with precision, singing Nazi songs at the tops of their voices. What fun they were having! They surely had no trouble about their identity. For a fleeting moment I envied them, wished that I too might share their carefree, secure togetherness.

The next moment I knew I was wrong. None of my friends would permit herself to think such a thought. I ticked them off in my mind: Anneke, Noortje, Nelletje, Marijke. No, I couldn't imagine any of them wanting to belong to the NSB.

But it's different for them, I thought defiantly. They were bound together too, in a way, by their patriotism and by their hatred of the oppressor. And what was more — they had a choice.

But I couldn't choose. What good was it to reject a group that wouldn't accept me even if I wanted to join?

Once again, as so often since the beginning of the occupation, I felt my Jewishness rising as an invisible barrier between myself and my friends. I knew that my friends would deny that such a barrier existed. They would rally around me just because it was against the rules. But I didn't want to be singled out. This accident of religious heritage — so unimportant to me before the war — now kept intruding.

Well, the one place where I still could be myself was in school. School hadn't changed. School went on as if there hadn't been a war and occupation. We had gone on double sessions because so many school buildings had been taken over by the Germans for their own purposes — but that was the only difference. We went through the old routine of spelling, grammar, and arithmetic lessons just as we had always done. It was comforting to know that no matter what happened in the outside world, in the classroom we would find the security of day-by-day routine.

But next year even school would change. This was our last year in elementary school. Already Anneke and I were worrying about our high school entrance exams. In Holland you can go to all kinds of different high schools. Anneke and I had been planning for years to go on to the Lyceum together. Both of her older sisters had graduated from that school and there had never been any question that Anneke would follow in their footsteps. I had been relieved when my parents had decided to let me apply to the Lyceum too.

When the day for taking our exams arrived, Anneke and I went together, clinging to each other for courage.

The Lyceum was a venerable old building of aged-darkened red brick. Generations of students had ridden their bicycles through the tunnel-like archway into the school courtyard and swarmed in and out of the heavy wooden doors. Their feet had worn a smooth path across the cobblestones of the yard and time had blackened the oldest of the initials carved into the old-fashioned desks in the high-ceilinged classrooms. The whole building seemed suffused with age and tradition, and both Anneke and I felt it as we walked out through the long wide corridors after the exam was over.

The test we had just taken would determine whether we would be allowed to attend this particular high school for the next six years. Six years! An eternity.

What if I didn't make it? Then I wouldn't be able to go to school with Anneke! She and I had been together since first grade. I had been new in the country then, shy and still a bit awkward with the Dutch language. But Anneke had taken me under her wing, helping me to adjust, defending me when other children teased me. I still depended on her to make plans and to have new ideas. Sometimes I wondered why Anneke put up with me.

For the next two weeks I hovered around the

mailbox. Then the big, stiff white envelope from the Lyceum arrived. It was an acceptance notice! Two minutes later I was on my way to Anneke's house. She waved her own letter at me the moment I entered her room. We ran to embrace each other. We were in!

Suddenly I couldn't wait for this school year to be over . . . for the next one to begin. I already thought of myself as a Lyceum student. Only the summer to live through.

It was a miserable summer. Anneke left to spend vacation with her grandparents in the south of Holland. Most of my other friends had travel plans too. But for me there would be no seashore vacation this summer. Jews were banned from all beach resorts.

I missed the beach — the smell of the sea, the feel of the wet sand squishing under my bare toes. Even the municipal swimming pool was off limits. NO JEWS ALLOWED said a big sign at the door.

The days crept by, the moments punctuated by no's: no beach . . . no pool . . . nothing to do. Nothing to do but to think about the new school and to play games with the time. My mother did it by inviting company — by filling our house with guests. We seemed to have guests all the time these days — for tea, for dinner, for an after-dinner chat.

"Doesn't she know there is a war on and rationing?" I muttered to Grannie as I got ready to set the table for guests for the third time that week.

"Our guests bring more in food and ration

coupons than they eat any day," Grannie laughed. But I wasn't convinced.

Day after day my mother came home from the stores with her string shopping bag half empty. Everything was in short supply. Eggs, butter, milk, cheese — Holland had always been a dairy country but whole herds of Dutch cattle had found their way to Germany by now. And the chickens and pigs had gone the same way.

Angrily I flung the tablecloth across the table, then headed for the buffet to get the silverware. The empty drawer suddenly reminded me that we no longer owned our best silver. Along with the heirloom candelabra and other family treasures, our silverware had been collected by the Germans "to help with the war effort." According to the Germans, Jews had no right to own silverware.

"It's only things, Rosie," my mother had said afterwards. But her engagement ring had been in one of the heavy suitcases my parents had carried to the collection depot that day, and her favorite gold and diamond pin, and the little string of seed pearls my other grandmother had sent me for my tenth birthday. Jews were not supposed to own jewelry either.

Yes, they were only things, but some of them had been in our family for generations. It scared me that people could just reach into our lives like this and take things away.

I looked back at the empty drawer. Well, our guests would have to do with kitchen knives and forks from now on. Not that they'd mind, any of them. They were pathetically grateful to share a meal at our table. Such a sorry collection of protégés my mother had gathered around her — lonely widows and widowers, some spinster cousins, a bachelor or two.

As food became more and more scarce, I resented their presence at our dinner table, even though I knew very well that the ration coupons and food gifts they brought made up for any amounts they consumed.

"Don't be selfish," my mother chided when I grumbled. "It's good to have friends, to share with friends, when times are hard."

"Don't spoil your mother's fun," my father told me with the special kind of smile he used when he and I shared some secret. "Your mother needs people around her, and this is the only kind of pleasure left to her these days."

Yes, we *were* playing games, my mother and I. For her it was guests, for me it was school. Games or make-believe to pretend that life wasn't really different.

Toward the end of August I received the first of a series of mailings from the Lyceum with book lists and various instructions to new students. Since Anneke was not due back in the city until shortly before school was to open, I decided to set out on my own to buy the textbooks I would need for my first high school year. No sense in waiting until all of the best second-hand books were sold out in the Lyceum book store. Besides I needed to have something to do.

The store was already crowded with students when I arrived. Many of them were obviously upperclassmen who moved familiarly among the tall bookshelves, calling out greetings to friends and to the sales people behind the counters. How mature and self-assured they seemed! I wondered if I too would look like this to a first-year student next year.

It was fun browsing from shelf to shelf, checking off selections from my long list of required books: music, botany, history, geography. . . . It was almost like a preview of the work I would do this next year. Some of the second-hand books were grimy with use, others seemed new and practically unused. I was glad I had come early.

Finally I had found all of my books. With the tall stack of volumes balanced in my arms I made my way to the cashier's desk. I never saw the tall blonde until we had collided just beyond the last bookshelf. Half of my books went bouncing to the floor.

"For heaven's sake, Carla!" I exclaimed. With so many strangers around, I had bumped into one of my elementary school classmates. I was glad to see her, even though Carla and I scarcely knew each other. In school Carla had moved with a different crowd.

Carla made no effort to help me retrieve my scattered books.

"Well, that's a surprise — seeing you here," she said loudly. "I didn't think you'd go to the trouble of buying books and all — for the short time, I mean."

"What do you mean?" The words were spoken before I had a chance to pull my wits together. Then the meaning sank in and I felt the color draining from my cheeks. Did Carla know something about the fate of Jewish students that I hadn't heard until now. I felt her staring at me. Wordlessly I went down on my knees and began to gather my wayward books. I couldn't trust my voice to say anything else right now.

Above my head, Carla was still talking.

"Oh, but I was sure you'd have heard," she protested. "I mean, everybody has been talking about it all summer — "

"Hush, Carla — how could you?" someone whispered urgently. Dejectedly I wondered whether everyone in the store had been listening to the exchange.

Without looking at Carla I got up and took my books to the cashier. I was glad that it took the man a long time to total up the amount because that gave me a chance to regain my composure.

When I turned to leave, Carla was still standing on the same spot. She was still staring at me. Gritting my teeth, I prepared to pass her, trying to walk as straight and proudly as possible. But Carla clutched at my arm.

"Please, Rosie, I meant no harm," she pleaded. "Really I didn't . . ."

"Sure, Carla." I was surprised at how calm I could be. "See you at school next week."

Then I fled from the store.

All the rest of that week I worried. But there were no further announcements and finally the first day of school arrived.

Anneke was back. We bicycled to the Lyceum together, feeling proud and important and a bit frightened. But the relief that I was actually starting at the Lyceum canceled out my earlier worries about meeting all those new people. I discovered that most of the other new students felt just as strange and lost as I did. Carla was in our classroom and she waved hesitatingly from her desk.

By the time school let out at four I had committed myself heart and soul to the staid and tradition-bound institution.

I belong here, I thought. I'm really here — a student — and this is my school. Now I am safe. They won't throw us out now that school has actually started. I'm safe for now — for this first year!

For the first time in months I stopped thinking about being different. It was as if the war and the occupation had never happened . . . as if it were peacetime again . . . as if I were not in a trap. Just geography and history and music and the daily chatter about teachers and boys. After two weeks I felt as if I had never been in another school.

Then, when we'd just started the third week of school, my homeroom teacher told me that I was wanted in the auditorium. She wouldn't tell me what it was all about.

Leaving my books in my desk, I headed down the stairs. Other students were coming from various directions but I didn't know any of them. I hadn't been in the school long enough.

I sat down by myself in one of the back rows of the auditorium, wondering what the principal wanted from us. He was pacing up and down nervously on the podium, watching as the students he had summoned filed into the hall.

Who were all these other students, and what had I to do with them? I scanned the unknown faces until I spotted one familiar one across the room. Tommy Baumann! His parents and mine were friends, and we had spent several summers together at the beach. I'd known that Tommy was at the Lyceum, but he was two years older than I and so far I hadn't run into him.

Tommy was whispering with some friends. They all looked frightened and upset. If I could only get across the hall to Tommy. Perhaps he'd tell me what was going on.

But it was too late. The principal had started to talk. His face looked strained and somber. He even had tears in his eyes. He spoke in short, uneven snatches as if he weren't quite sure of his voice. And he hadn't finished his first sentence before I knew what I had in common with all the other students in the hall. We were all Jewish. And without really listening to his words I knew what he was going to say.

Snatches of his speech got through to me . . . a word here and there. He spoke about terrible times and sad moments . . . about everybody in Holland feeling deprived with us.

The Lyceum would always feel the loss of so many fine students, he said. "Someday you will return — we will welcome you back with open arms. But now we must part. My heart is heavy as I tell you this news. But I have no choice."

He said more, but I stopped listening. I didn't

want to hear more. In spite of all the rumors, in spite of all my worrying, I was stunned and dazed by the news. I looked around. How were the others taking it? Were they taken by surprise too? Some girls were crying. The boys walked out of the auditorium pale and tight-lipped.

Near the door I caught up with Tommy Baumann and I grabbed him by the arm.

"Oh, Tommy, isn't it awful?" I blurted out. "I can't bear it. I just hate to leave this school."

Tommy recoiled almost visibly. Two bright spots appeared on his sallow cheeks.

"Oh, let's just not talk about it," he almost shouted at me. "How would you know — you just started! How would you know how I feel about leaving the school!"

He pushed roughly past me, his shoulders hunched into his cardigan. Stung, I stared after him. I had never really liked Tommy Baumann very much — but this was not like him at all. I'd never known him to be rude.

But then, I wasn't quite myself either, I thought, as I trudged up the stairs back to my classroom to get my belongings. I was moving and talking and walking, but I had this strange hollow feeling inside of me as if I weren't really there at all — as if I were watching myself from the outside and seeing a stranger. The homeroom was empty — the other students had gone on to their usual round of classes. In some ways I was glad that Anneke wasn't there to see me gathering up my things.

With my books in my arms, I hesitated at the

door. What else was there to do? What about my half-finished drawing in art class, or the book-ends I'd started to make in woodworking shop? Should I go and get them or leave them there? What about the results of last week's math test? Now I'd never know how I did on it. And the story my Dutch literature teacher had started to read in class yesterday. I'd never find out the ending.

Should I go and say good-bye to any of my teachers? A few of the older students seemed to be making the rounds. No, I couldn't bear to face any of them. And what good would it be, anyway? To most of them I was still only a name, a new face they'd barely learned to recognize. They would remove my name from the roll-call book and that would be the end of it. In another day or so it would be as if I'd never been to the Lyceum at all.

Chapter 3

NOW THERE WERE to be stars sewn on our clothes to show who we were.

The stars were printed on coarse yellow cloth — a garish yellow — with the Star of David outlined in thick black lines. In the center of each star, in even thicker black lines, the word Jew had been printed in mock-Hebrew type. They were to be worn sewn on our clothes — over the heart, as Grannie said — at all times, indoors or out.

My mother had gone to buy our allotment of yellow stars at the distribution center, giving up precious clothing coupons in exchange. Now the long strips of yellow cloth from which we had to cut out the individual stars lay unrolled on our dining room table. I stared at them with loathing.

"The Star of David — such a lovely symbol — and look how it is being misused," Grannie sighed as she carefully snipped along the printed outlines to free the six-pointed stars from the excess cloth. "This will unravel right away," she complained. "We'll have to hem around each star before we can use them."

Such a waste of time and effort and material!

"It's barbaric," I muttered, liking the sound of the word. "That's what it is — utterly barbaric!"

"And not even original!" my father said, joining the conversation for the first time. "Did you know, Rosie, that they used a yellow patch in the Middle Ages to identify Jews? The Third Reich simply took a giant step backwards."

"Oh, how can you think about history at a time like this!" I said irritably, glaring at my father.

"I'm just trying to put this in perspective," he said.

"Well, I won't wear them," I said. "I won't go out on the street, wearing a thing like that."

"Of course you'll wear them, Rosemarie," my mother said. "We'll all wear them because we cannot break the law."

"I won't go out on the street, then," I said obstinately.

"You can't stay indoors for the rest of the war, darling," my mother said reasonably. "Don't worry — people won't be staring at you, I promise you that. You'll see — everybody will be most sympathetic."

"I don't want sympathy — I want to be like

everyone else," I cried, storming out of the room.

In the end of course I went back, feeling foolish. Deep inside I knew very well that part of my mother's forced cheerfulness was just a device to shield me. I was old enough to understand and recognize what she was doing. In her eyes I was still child enough to be spared unpleasant truths.

When the first time came to go out with the star, I hesitated for long moments in the hallway. Twice I opened the front door and closed it again. Desperately I tried to think of something I had forgotten upstairs, just to postpone the moment of stepping out into the street, of being exposed, marked with that hateful emblem.

"You must wear it like a badge of courage," Grannie told me. "Walk straight, hold your head up high, and people will show you respect."

Courage! I suppose I was a coward at heart. Even though I hated myself for doing it, I hid the star every chance I had — behind a pile of school books or a package that I carried, anything to pretend the star wasn't there.

Grannie had been right about the reaction of other people. Everybody we knew disregarded the star. Friends, neighbors, even strangers, approached us with a friendly word, a kind gesture. But I still didn't want to be singled out, not even out of kindness or pity. Especially pity.

For the first time in the six months since I'd had to leave the Lyceum I was almost glad that

I now attended a Jewish school. At least here I was not different from the others. We all wore the yellow badge and we all shared the same lot.

In the beginning I had hated that new makeshift school. Classes were held in a private house where groups of students would meet in all available nooks and crannies, including the garden, weather permitting. I'd sit in one of those classes among a lot of strangers, trying to remember what Anneke or Carla would be doing at the Lyceum just then. I still knew the schedule by heart. Dutch literature first on Monday mornings and then music and geography. We had been studying the Indonesian Islands. Probably by now the class would have gone as far as Borneo. . . .

Once, when my own school was closed for some reason, I walked over to the Lyceum just to see it again. From across the street I looked up at the age-blackened structure, at the rows and rows of deep-set windows marching across the brick facade. The windows seemed to stare back at me like so many expressionless eyes. Swarms of students spilled out of the wide double doors. It was recess. Their exuberant voices drifted across the open square. Already I felt quite remote from them. At that moment I felt remote even from Anneke. For the first time it occurred to me that I might never return.

But now that I wore the yellow star, I avoided the Lyceum. Even the relatively short walk between home and my new school was an ordeal.

I envied the students who really wore their badges with pride and with a sense of history and their own religious convictions. But I felt as far removed from them as I now felt separated from my old friends.

The worst moment every morning came when I had to cross Euterpe Straat half a block away from my house. Here the Gestapo had taken over two high school buildings facing each other across a quiet square. Very soon this pleasant tree-lined street became a center of terror. Uniformed, jackbooted SS officers could be seen in greater numbers here than anywhere else in the city and many people brought in for questioning were never heard of again. People who didn't need to go near them avoided the vicinity of these buildings.

But we couldn't avoid a place less than a block away from our house. The presence of the Gestapo hung like a dark cloud over the entire neighborhood. And with the introduction of the yellow star the feeling became worse. I could sense the Gestapo guard looking at me each time I walked down the block. I tried to pretend I didn't notice, but I could feel myself quake inside.

One day, early in May, our doorbell rang loudly and long. I had just come home from school and I was still in the hall, my school bag in hand. I beat my mother to the door.

There were two men on our doorstep dressed in civilian clothes. Yes? I asked, but they didn't answer. They pushed their way past me. Security policemen, I thought before they even flashed their identity cards.

My mother met them and behind her back motioned to me to go upstairs. My father wasn't home and I hated to leave her alone, but somehow I didn't dare disobey. I withdrew to the upper landing, hanging over the banister and straining to hear what was going on.

I couldn't hear too well, but the bits of conversation I caught added up all too clearly: . . . need for a Jewless area . . . expropriation of the house . . . eviction orders. . . .

Then the voices drew nearer. I heard footsteps on the stairs and I shrank back into my room.

From room to room the men went, making notes about our furnishings, commenting sarcastically about our possessions and reminding us that soon these things would no longer be in the hands of "dirty Jewish pigs."

Then they were in my room, coldly disregarding my presence. Insolently they looked around, touching my things, peeking into my closet. I stood stiffly against the wall, waiting for the inspection to be over. One of the men went over to my desk, glanced through my books, picked up the glass paperweight my parents had once brought me as a souvenir from Paris. He shook it and with him I watched the make-believe snowflakes drifting across the tiny Eiffel tower. He sauntered around the room, his eyes fastening on the pink silk comforter, which was folded on the foot of my bed. He touched it, feeling the satiny texture.

"Pink silk," he sneered. "She won't have it so good after this. No more pink silk comforters for Jewish brats."

I noticed that my mother's hands were clenched tightly during the onslaught, but she remained silent no matter what they said. To me, the fact that these two rude men spoke Dutch made their arrogance even harder to bear.

Finally they left, voicing dire threats about what would happen to us if we dared to take anything out of the house besides two suitcases apiece of clothing and personal belongings. They gave us three days to vacate the house.

The moment they were gone I rushed toward my mother and we clung to each other, in silence. I guess we were so relieved that they were gone that we couldn't even start to think about the future. But then the truth of what had happened sank in. Three days! Three days from now we would be homeless — out on the street with just the few belongings we could carry away!

"Where shall we go?" Grannie cried when she heard the news. "And what shall we take? Clothing, food, bedding — everything is important. But how can we carry it all?"

"We have three days — we'll find a way," my mother soothed, just as she had comforted me earlier. "Someone will come to our rescue — we'll find a roof over our heads, even if it's just a temporary one."

We started to pack. Packing became an obsession. How do you choose among possessions piled up in a lifetime? We all fluttered about, searching closets and cupboards, rummaging in drawers and trunks. I was sent to fetch and carry.

"Rosemarie, bring up the supplies of sugar and sardines and canned milk from the basement. They're more important than clothes," my mother ordered.

"What about the pickled eggs?" Grannie demanded. Early in the war she had spent hours in the kitchen preserving eggs in a special liquid and storing them in large glass jars on the basement shelves.

But there was no way of taking those precious eggs along. They would have to be left behind along with more durable treasures.

"Remember, we'll have to carry these things ourselves," my father kept reminding us. "Clothing and some food — that's all we can manage."

"What about my records?" I asked. "I just got these two last month."

"Darling, what good are records without a record player?" my father asked gently.

I put the records back on the shelf, stifling an impulse to drop and smash the whole lot of them. I felt like running around the house, smashing everything we couldn't take with us. Why should we leave it all to the Nazis? But I didn't dare. Perhaps those hateful men had noted down my records too on their inventory lists.

In the kitchen I found my mother sitting on the floor, shuffling around a pile of pots and pans. She looked tired and her movements were slow. All of a sudden she began shoving all of the pots back into the cupboard.

"It's no use," she sighed. "We can't carry them anyway. I'm not even going to try to decide."

She picked up a box of old letters she had looked through earlier.

"Let's burn those in the furnace," she said. "There is no time to sort them and I don't want to leave them here."

In spite of the watchful Gestapo guard across the way there were a few small keepsakes we did manage to smuggle out of the house. We were aided by the particular way our two-family house was constructed. The Dijkmans, who lived in the upper two stories, had their own entrance right next to our front door. A long, steep stairway led to their apartment. The space between our two entranceways was linked by a small utility tunnel. Trapdoors, each hidden by a set-in doormat, gave access to this low and narrow space.

At night, under cover of the tightly closed blackout curtains, our two families worked feverishly to transfer such cherished mementos as photo albums, favorite knickknacks, some valuable first editions from our bookcase. Since I was the smallest of us all, I was elected to crawl back and forth through the dusty passage, passing on the items handed down to me. I tried not to think about the spiderwebs and mouse droppings which cluttered the dark little passageway. Luckily I was too busy to worry much about it or to agonize about causes and consequences. Anyway, there was a certain grim satisfaction in knowing that we were cheating the Germans right under their very noses.

On the third morning, my mother called me when the sun was barely up. There was still so much to do — and so little time. We scurried around, closing suitcases, tidying rooms. When my mother seemed to be running out of things for me to do, I escaped. "I'm going up for a last look," I said, dashing up the stairs before my mother had a chance to say no. I walked from room to room, saying good-bye.

In my room I opened the deep walk-in closet that had once held most of my toys, my records, my special treasures. Piled up in one corner were all the dolls I hadn't touched for years. I picked up Trudy with the yellow hair. She stared blankly back at me with her china blue glass eyes and when I tilted her to put her back on the pile she startled me with her high-pitched, plaintive cry. I ran my fingers over the cold, smooth cardboard surface of a stack of games and then my hand brushed against something soft and warm and furry. Fluffy! Without looking I knew that it was the cuddly plush dog I had loved threadbare as a toddler and had kept year after year long after my other baby toys had been discarded. For a moment I was tempted to rescue him — to smuggle him somehow out of the house, hidden in my suitcase. No! There were more important things to carry with me. Anyway, hadn't I long since felt far too grown-up for any of the toys in this cupboard? Hadn't I? Quickly I closed the closet.

At the window I took one last long look at the sunny garden below. The tulips were in bloom along the edges of the flower beds, the gnarled branches of the old walnut tree were bright with young green leaves, and the tall chestnut tree with its crown of white candles competed with the pale cascade of blossoms on the slender lilac bush below.

Downstairs, in the living room, my mother sat next to the pile of closed suitcases and tied-up bundles we expected to take with us. She looked tired and somehow defeated. It suddenly dawned on me how awful it must be for my mother to leave behind all the things she had so lovingly collected over the years to build her home. It was more than just the loss of a roof over our heads, more than the worry about our future. There were memories in all those objects for my mother — just as those old toys upstairs were memories for me. A moment ago I had wanted to run to my mother, to be comforted for my own loss. Now, suddenly, I wanted to comfort her.

She didn't give me a chance. She was running her hand through her hair, her mind again on things that had to be done.

"You'd better take care of Puss now, Rosemarie," she reminded me.

I'd almost forgotten about this particular painful farewell. Puss had been with me since he'd been a black and white ball of a kitten. Now a proud tomcat, he had grown almost too heavy for me to carry. I found him on his favorite sunny spot in front of the French doors in the living room and I lifted him to my lap to cuddle him one last time. The Nederburghs at the end of the block had offered to keep Puss for the time being, since we certainly couldn't be burdened with a cat just now. I was glad that Puss could stay among his familiar backyard fences, but it was hard to give him up.

Cradling Puss in my arms, I started off toward his new home, using the shortcut through the backyards. Mrs. Nederburgh received Puss tenderly, but Puss didn't want to stay in her arms. He struggled, twisted, and he turned his head toward me. How could I leave him with strangers when he wanted to be with me?

Mrs. Nederburgh saw how I felt.

"I'll take good care of him, Rosie," she promised. "I'll buy fish heads for him as often as I can get them, and I promise you that I'll keep him safe from harm."

Mrs. Nederburgh put down Puss and took me in her arms. "Good luck, Rosemarie," she whispered.

I ran back through the gardens, swallowing hard to force back the tears.

And then there was no more time and we had to leave. With our bundles and suitcases we stood on the street, trying to gather our belongings as best as we could.

"Thank God for Harry Brouwer," my mother sighed. Mr. Brouwer, one of my mother's protégés, had offered to take us all in for the first few days.

"Didn't I always tell you, Rosemarie: One hand washes the other," my mother added. "Well, isn't it good to have friends?"

I didn't answer, but I hoped that Mr. Brouwer hadn't guessed that I hadn't always appreciated his company.

We started out, walking slowly, hampered by our bulky load. Halfway down the block my mother paused to look back. Already a truck had pulled up to our door and several men were busy carrying pieces of furniture out of the house.

"Look, they have the inlaid chest," my mother said with a quaver in her voice.

"Don't look back," my father said quietly.

Chapter 4

WE STAYED with Mr. Brouwer for two weeks. Then we moved again—to a rooming house.

"Three rooms with kitchenette," my mother reported when she came back from inspecting our new quarters. "A bit cramped, but we'll be together and that's what counts. And you'll have a room of your own again, Rosie. With a balcony."

The rooming house was one of a whole crescent-shaped block of similar buildings, all owned by a strong-minded lady of French Huguenot descent. It was quite in character for Mrs. Dubois to have taken us in at that particular time and under those particular circumstances. Mrs. Dubois would do anything to thwart the Nazis. We were only one of several Jewish families who had found refuge under her roof.

I had to admit that the new place was pleasant and I liked my new room. We were not really very far away from our old neighborhood. A five-minute bicycle ride — not more. But we were no longer permitted to use bicycles or streetcars.

As far as I was concerned, we might as well have moved to the other end of the world. Until then I had still seen most of my old friends around the neighborhood. But now even Anneke stopped being truly a part of my life. At first she came to see me a few times, full of news about Mme. Leclerque, the French teacher we had both hated, or about that funny old Mrs. Pots who lived down the block from my old house. But there was something awkward about these meetings. It was as if after the first few minutes we didn't quite know what to talk about. Perhaps I didn't really want to hear about the old neighbors and her doings at the Lyceum, nor tell about my own life in the odd, makeshift school. I don't know, but something was happening between us, and I think Anneke felt it too. She came less and less often, stayed only briefly, pleading a heavy homework schedule. Finally her visits stopped completely.

Her absence left a gap in my life. In my new school I had been slow at making new friends. The girls in my class were pleasant enough and I enjoyed talking to them in school, but there really wasn't much we could do together after school hours. We couldn't go to the movies or the skating rink or the municipal swimming pool. The ice-cream parlors were barred to us as were the libraries and the museums. Most of the things I used to do with my old friends were no longer possible if you were Jewish. Even visiting each other was difficult because our homes were scattered in many directions. And I was too shy to invite anyone to my home.

Julie came closest to being my new best friend. She lived near me and we walked to school together. Julie was older than I and I learned many things from her — about boys, about clothes, about sex. But I couldn't share my thoughts and feelings with her the way I had done with Anneke. Julie rarely stopped talking long enough to listen to someone else.

One day Mrs. Dubois stopped me on the street in front of the house.

"There's someone I'd like you to meet," she told me in her firm but always slightly breathless voice. "Her name is Eleanor. You two will like each other. You're a bit younger than she is, but that doesn't matter. She spends too much time with older people. What Eleanor needs is young company."

She explained that Eleanor and her parents were German refugees who, like us, had found shelter in one of Mrs. Dubois' houses. I learned that Eleanor was nineteen, that she spoke very little Dutch, and that Mrs. Dubois was happy to find someone young who could speak German. It was typical of Mrs. Dubois that she left for the last the most salient fact about Eleanor.

"She is handicapped, you know," she told me the day we walked over to Eleanor's house. "Blind and deaf. Some disease when she was quite young. But she is a remarkable girl. After a while, you'll hardly notice."

I had an impulse to run away. There was enough unhappiness around me as it was — I didn't think I could face someone with such a handicap. But Mrs. Dubois had me firmly in tow and there was no escape.

Eleanor was a slim girl with short brown hair and unbelievably large but oddly unfocused eyes. She was sitting at a desk in her room, touch-typing on a large, old-fashioned typewriter. She sat up very straight and her eyes seemed to stare right in front of her at the blank wall behind her desk.

As her mother opened her door and led us into the room, Eleanor suddenly stopped typing. She turned around and looked toward the door as if she could see us.

"Mother?" she asked. She spoke slowly and with difficulty.

"Can she hear us?" I whispered, surprised.

"She senses our presence," Eleanor's mother said. "She even recognizes people by their steps. Vibrations, I guess."

She crossed over to the desk and took Eleanor's hand in hers. With her other hand she started a rapid tapping into the girl's open palm.

"It's a finger - alphabet," Mrs. Dubois explained. "She is probably telling Eleanor that you are here and describing you to her."

Eleanor seemed to "listen" intently. Then she asked some questions in a deep, husky voice, but I couldn't understand her because her speech was slurred. Her mother seemed to understand her perfectly.

"Eleanor would like to shake hands with you," she said.

Reluctantly I let her lead me toward the blind girl.

"Just take her hand," she urged.

Eleanor was holding out her hand to me and I grasped it and held it for a moment. Eleanor was smiling, but she looked past me, slightly to the left of my face.

"I'm glad to meet you," she said carefully, so carefully that even I could understand.

Afterwards we had tea in the other room. Eleanor's father, a tall, white-haired man, sat next to his daughter, her hand in his. As we talked, he constantly translated our conversation to her through rapid tapping of the finger alphabet. I stared at Eleanor in fascination. She was taking part in the conversation, laughing her husky laugh at the right moments and asking questions in her slow and careful speech.

"Please come often," Eleanor's mother told me when we left. "We'll teach you the finger alphabet. It will be so nice for Eleanor to talk to someone young."

How could I say no? It was something Mrs. Dubois wanted me to do, and after everything she had done for us, I couldn't refuse. But I still felt awkward about being with Eleanor. I never knew what to tap into her hand and besides I'd never been very good at spelling in German. It was easiest to read something to her from some book she couldn't obtain in braille. At least there the words were in front of me and even though it went slowly, I was doing something useful.

I kept coming, and suddenly I found it easy to understand Eleanor's speech and she became a friend.

I never stopped being surprised by her. How could she joke and laugh and be cheerful when she couldn't hear or see and her world was bounded almost entirely by the four walls of her tiny room? Sometimes I forgot and complained to her about the things I couldn't do anymore and how hemmed in I felt because so many places were closed to me now. Afterwards I'd feel ashamed.

But Eleanor had no self-pity. She had learned to live with her affliction. She accepted her limitations. And she didn't permit her physical prison to shut her away from the world outside. She reached out by reading any book in braille she could lay her hands on. And on her old typewriter with the braille keyboard and regular type she pounded out dozens of letters each week to an astonishingly large circle of friends scattered around half the globe. They wrote back to her — letters punched out on small braille slates so that she could read them for herself.

"What do you find to write about all the time?" I asked her once. Eleanor laughed. "Oh, about the things I read and hear. And I tell my friends news about each other."

"About me too?"

"Certainly about you. You'd be surprised how

many of my friends know about you by now. And they all think you are very nice."

"Did you tell them how bad my spelling is, too?" I asked, suddenly embarrassed.

When school closed for vacation, I saw even more of Eleanor. Otherwise there wasn't much for me to do. I thought longingly of the swimming pool and the tennis courts in the park. And then I remembered that my tennis racket had stayed behind in our house.

Sometimes Julie and I went for walks or we listened to records at her house. But one day, when I went to see her, her house was dark and shuttered. No one answered the door. Had Julie's family been arrested? Or gone into hiding? There was no one to ask.

More and more public places and stores were closed to Jews during the next few summer weeks. Now I accompanied my mother and Grannie once a week to the distant open-air market set up especially for Jewish shoppers. The rough wooden trestle tables, buzzing with flies, held the sorry array of wilted cabbages, stale bread, and shriveled potatoes Jews were permitted to buy. Most times we returned home with our coupons for meat or dairy products still unused.

I did a lot of reading that summer and what I missed most was the lending library. The neighbors brought books to me, but that wasn't the same as browsing among the shelves, picking out exciting-looking titles for myself. I was reading *Gone with the Wind* that summer — luckily a nice long book — and all during June and July

I suffered with Scarlett O'Hara and Melanie. It was really much easier to worry about the American Civil War — distant in time and place — than to concentrate on the present.

However, there were things that I couldn't shut out by reading. The call-up letters, for example. Jewish boys and girls in their late teens and early twenties began receiving these official letters early in June — letters instructing them to report to the Amsterdam railroad station on a certain day to be sent to Polish labor camps. "To help the war effort" the letters stated.

We knew many families that were affected. Grannie, who still went out regularly to play bridge with some of her old friends, usually was the one to bring the bad news.

"Imagine, Tommy Baumann was called to go," she reported after one of her bridge afternoons.

"My God, I never realized that boy was sixteen!" My mother looked startled. "The last time I saw him he was just a little boy."

"He won't go, of course," Grannie added. "Everybody has advised the Baumanns to let the boy disappear — go into hiding. I suppose they'll find a way, but poor Helene Baumann is beside herself with worry."

I only half listened to the rest of the conversation. I still remembered the look on Tommy's face the day we were told that we had to leave the Lyceum. And before that day, during those carefree prewar summers, when we were both small and Tommy had thrown sand at me on the beach. It was hard to believe that Tommy was considered grown-up enough to be sent all by himself to a labor camp. It was frightening too.

Tommy wasn't the only one to "submerge" after receiving the call-up letter. Many young people disappeared. The Dutch resistance movement rallied splendidly. Here at last was something they could do to help the Jews in their country.

Furiously, the Germans sent up more call-up letters. Then they began to arrest people at random — anywhere, on the streets or by ringing doorbells at Jewish homes.

Several times Mrs. Dubois came to warn us to stay indoors on certain days. It was then that we knew she and her family were active in the Dutch resistance movement. Through the underground she sometimes had news about intended raiding forays. "Razzias" these dragnet raids were called. The people caught in them were held, bullied, and questioned and, if their age was right, they were sent off to Poland instead of those who had disobeyed the official call. Others were sent home, relieved but disturbed by what they had seen.

"I'm so glad you're not older," my mother kept telling me. "So far we are lucky — you are too young, Grannie and we are too old. They don't need us in their labor battalions."

"Then why are you packing those rucksacks?" I asked her. I had watched her getting them ready when she thought I wasn't looking — one rucksack for each of us — stuffed tightly with warm clothing, flashlights and soap, sardines, cocoa, and canned condensed milk.

"Just to be safe. Let's hope we'll never have to use them," my mother said, not quite looking at me.

June slipped into July and then into August. It was a hot summer — unusually hot for Amsterdam. Even the air seemed oppressive. But at least August meant that summer was nearly over. Just a few weeks more and school would start again. At least school would give me something to do.

It was another very hot morning when Mrs. Dubois came in with a new razzia warning.

"They have started in quite a distant neighborhood, but you'd better be careful just in case," she said.

"I want you to stay home, Rosie," my mother warned. I nodded absentmindedly. I had a book to finish anyway.

We were sitting at lunch when the raucous siren of the dreaded Gestapo car sounded — first in the distance, then closer down the street. We listened in frozen silence, willing them to pass our house. No — the siren had stopped. We heard a screeching of brakes and the slamming of car doors. The police were outside — right in front of our house.

"Rosemarie, go upstairs to your room," my mother said. "You and Grannie." Her face had gone white and she was listening intently to the footsteps on the street below. A moment later we heard the doorbell ring.

"Go, Rosemarie, quickly," my mother said again.

I wanted to argue, but the strained look on

my parents' faces made me hold back. Grannie was already at the door. Reluctantly, I followed my grandmother up the stairs.

From the entrance hall we could hear the voices of our downstairs neighbor and of a Dutch NSB officer — the Dutch version of the Gestapo.

"Brenner — Charles and Louise Brenner."

He was asking for us by name! Our neighbor hesitated for a long moment but then she stammered a reply and I heard the heavy footsteps coming up the stairs.

Through a crack in Grannie's door I heard my mother asking if she might change into different clothes.

"A few minutes," the man muttered. I was afraid to move, to breathe. I waited to be called — for some signs from my parents to tell me what was going on. But now even the voices ceased. There was only silence. Then I heard my parents walking down the stairs. I ran to a front window. In spite of the hot August weather, my parents had changed into ski pants and ski boots and were carrying heavy coats! The sight of them getting into the police van dressed so strangely for a summer day made my mouth go dry with sudden fear.

"They are coming back, aren't they, Grannie?" I cried out in panic.

"Of course, they'll be back," Grannie murmured, but she sounded as if she were trying to convince herself.

Our neighbor, who had come upstairs to comfort me and Grannie was more reassuring.

"Of course they'll be home. Your parents are over forty, Rosemarie. The Germans have never kept people past their twenties. They'll be home tonight."

But they did not come home that night. Instead a message came from the Jewish Council. It seemed the Germans were not freeing anybody this time. It didn't matter how old they were. Tomorrow the group would be sent to Westerbork, the transit camp in the province of Drente, near the German frontier. From there they would be sent to Poland.

"What will happen to them there? Why can't I go with them?" Frantically I grabbed at the messenger's arm, half afraid that he too would suddenly vanish before my eyes.

"They want you to stay here with your grandmother," he said. "Your parents think that would be the best for you. The Germans are not looking for children or old people. Your parents will be reunited with you when the war is over."

Dully I watched my grandmother hand the man a satchel of clothing and other necessities for my parents. His administrative duties allowed him to pass in and out of the Gestapo headquarters. He turned to me before leaving.

"I will tell your parents that you and your grandmother are bearing up well."

Bearing up well! What a joke. How did he know what I was feeling?

"Don't be scared, Rosie. I'll take care of you," Grannie promised after the man had gone. Through my tears I looked at Grannie. She seemed to have aged by ten years that afternoon and she looked so frail that a gust of wind might have blown her away. Yet she had a determined look on her face.

How could Grannie take care of me? Grannie, who got sick so often and who needed so much help. I'll have to watch out for *her*, I told myself.

That night the heat wave broke with a violent rainstorm. Snug in my bed, I wondered if my parents were safely under shelter or if they were still detained in the open Gestapo yard.

I should have stayed with them, I thought for the fiftieth time. I shouldn't have let my mother send me upstairs.

Now they were gone, without even a last kiss, a final embrace.

"I'll never see them again," I thought as the rain pattered on the sidewalk below. Usually I liked to listen to the sound of rain when I was in bed. But this evening the rain had a low, mournful sound.

I finally fell asleep, and I slept late the next morning, not really wanting to awake. When I did, I heard friends and neighbors talking to Grannie. Vaguely I heard Grannie talking about ways to prevent my parents' immediate deportation—about people to be seen, avenues to be explored. But there was so little time—no time, really. They were to leave before daybreak the next day, and there was nothing anyone could do except hope that the war would end soon.

That third night there was no rain to keep me awake, but I tossed and turned, trying to keep myself from sleeping. I wanted to be awake when the time came for my parents to leave

— to think of them during their last few hours on Dutch soil.

I guess I was just too exhausted to manage it. I fell asleep long before dawn, and when I woke up, still feeling dizzy with fatigue, it was too late: The train bearing my parents eastward would have left long ago.

I found Grannie in my parents' room downstairs, slowly going through the familiar motions of making breakfast. Neither of us was hungry, but we had to eat. We faced each other silently across the breakfast table and I suppose we made an odd pair: an old woman, who had seen too much and who seemed beyond tears; and a girl, who had cried so much that her eyes were dry.

The phone rang, shrilly and loud, on the table in the corner. I watched listlessly as Grannie went slowly to answer it. I heard Grannie's tired hello and then a sharp intake of breath as her sagging shoulders suddenly straightened and her face lit up.

"Where are you, what happened, where are you now?" Grannie cried into the telephone, her words tumbling over each other in her excitement. "Yes, yes, I'll tell the child. Oh, thank God, thank God, thank God. Yes, yes, I understand."

I was half out of my chair.

"Mother? Daddy?" I whispered, not quite daring to voice my question. Grannie nodded, as she replaced the receiver with shaking hands.

Chapter 5

GRANNIE SAT DOWN HEAVILY in the big easy chair next to the phone. Her face was ashen and her lips trembled.

"What is it, Grannie?" I almost shouted. "What did they say? Where are they now?"

"They are coming home," Grannie said, almost as if she were talking to herself. "Not to stay — just for one night. They are coming for you, Rosie. To take you to the camp."

Now it was my turn to sink back into my chair. My parents were coming home! They were coming to get me. I would be with them again soon!

"Are you sure?" I whispered, not quite trusting what I had heard.

Grannie nodded.

"You'll go with them tomorrow," she said again.

"Oh, I want to go, I want to go," I cried.

"I'm glad they didn't leave without me. I don't mind going to the camp."

Grannie didn't answer. She sat very still, her hands taut on the arms of the chair.

Why isn't she happy with me? I wondered. And then I understood. For Grannie there was nothing to rejoice about. When I left, Grannie would be all alone.

Remorsefully, I rushed to her side.

"Please don't be sad, Grannie," I pleaded.

Grannie took my hand into hers.

"God protect you, darling," she whispered.

Then we went to work. All morning long we shuffled my possessions around, trying to stuff the maximum amount of warm clothing into my rucksack.

"It gets cold out there in Poland," Grannie said each time she added another sweater or another pair of heavy socks. "Never mind those dresses or that frilly blouse. It's the winter things that may have to last you a long, long time."

Now the rucksack lay strapped and buckled on my bed and across it, tied into a neat sausage shape, my pink quilted comforter was rolled up tightly with the blankets from my bed. Tonight I would sleep with borrowed blankets. These were the things, the only things, I would take tomorrow into my new and unknown life.

On a sudden impulse I picked up a notebook and a small sketchbook from my desk. I had to shove hard to get them deep into my rucksack between my clothes. But how could I go away without something along on which to write or draw?

Afterwards I went to see Mr. Hemelrijk. He used to own a large, modern beauty parlor, but now carried on his trade for his Jewish customers in the back room of his own apartment. Mother had given orders for me to cut my braids. A short bob is easier to keep clean, she said.

I felt odd as I settled down in the high barber's chair and submitted to the ritual of wraparound sheets and towels. In the mirror, I watched as Mr. Hemelrijk combed out my braids and applied his flashing scissors. Chunks of brown hair slid across my draped shoulders and fell to the floor. I closed my eyes. I really didn't want to see it happen. But when I looked again, the shock was worse.

"What a shame," Mr. Hemelrijk muttered as he shaped the wispy remnants of my hair. I kept silent. I remembered how long it had taken me to grow my hair long enough for those braids. But it doesn't matter, I told myself. Nothing matters, except that Mother and Daddy are coming home today.

While Mr. Hemelrijk went to find change, I watched Mrs. Hemelrijk sweep the last few fluffs of brown hair into her dustpan.

"You look very pretty with your short hairdo, Rosie," she said.

I gave her a wan smile. She was a nice woman and she was trying to make me feel better. But I wasn't fooled.

All the way home, each time I happened to catch my reflection in the plate-glass window, I was shocked anew. Like a round-faced cherub, I thought, if there were brown-haired cherubs.

Back home, I found Grannie darting about, trying to do twenty things at the same time. She was cooking soup and baking cookies, sorting clothes and gathering odds and ends she felt my parents might need at the camp. She was so preoccupied, she didn't even seem to notice my hair.

Poor Grannie doesn't dare to stop working because she doesn't want time to think how quiet tomorrow will be, I thought.

I tried to help, but while she worked, friends and relatives who had heard the news began to drift in to wait with us for my parents. By mid-afternoon I felt as if I had never done anything in my life but wait. Time lay suspended. I was trapped in time. I couldn't bear the hushed, aimless conversations of the waiting adults any longer so I fled upstairs to the sanctuary of my room.

From my balcony I could see as far as the end of the block. The street was utterly quiet. It was so still I thought I could hear my own heart beating. Where are they? I thought. Why don't they come? Why is it taking them so long?

I began to notice all kinds of crazy things on the street — the way the cracks in the sidewalk were casting their own shadows in the late after-noon sun and that the streetlight on the corner wasn't quite straight. After a while my eyes started to hurt from staring so hard at that one corner. Twice I heard footsteps approaching in the distance, then fading away along some other street.

Please let it be them, I prayed when I heard steps again.

Suddenly my parents were there below me, walking wearily down the block. They still wore the same clothes they had on when they were arrested, but now these were dusty and crumpled and out of shape.

I practically flew down the stairs two and three steps at a time, shouting: "They're here, they're here!" I struggled with the front door. It wouldn't open fast enough. Then I was in their arms, clinging to both of them at the same time, as we all sobbed and laughed and talked in turn.

Behind me I heard Grannie's slow steps coming down the stairs. I heard her stop to pick up the ashtray I had brushed off the hall table in my haste, and then she too moved in for her welcoming embrace.

I yielded my place in my mother's arms with reluctance. All the way up the stairs I clung to her hand, listening to Grannie's rapid chatter.

"I'll have to wash those clothes right away," she was saying. "You'll want them tomorrow and they'll need time to dry. And you look starved, absolutely starved. There is warm food on the stove — you can eat right away."

For the first time since she had come in, my mother's face broke into a smile.

"First things first, Mother," she said gently. "What I need most of all is a hot bath. I've been dreaming of a hot tub for the last three days. At least, when I wasn't thinking of you and Rosemarie!"

She pulled me close again and for the first time she noticed my hair.

"Oh, darling — you look lovely. I always did like you best with short hair. Look, Charles, isn't that pretty?"

"I thought you looked different — older or something," Daddy said. "But I like it, Kitten, I like it very much."

How absurd it all was, this conversation about my hair out here on the upstairs landing, with all the friends and relatives crowded in the open doorway and spilling out into the hall! Were my parents pleased or dismayed to find such a large welcoming committee in their room?

My mother escaped right away to the peace and quiet of the bathroom, where Grannie was filling the tub for her. I trailed after my father, who circulated from group to group, heedless of his fatigue. It was like a party, a strange kind of celebration, half happy and half sad. Even Grannie acted like the hostess at a party, urging cold drinks and cake on people as if she'd never heard of wartime shortages and ration cards.

Mother emerged from the bathroom looking fresher and more relaxed. More like her old, normal self. Gone was the defeated sag of her shoulders, the strained look in her eyes. In her long blue robe, her naturally wavy blond hair still slightly damp at the ends, Mother seemed as much herself as she might any morning after her bath. Perhaps it was all just a nightmare, I thought wistfully, a dream from which I would awaken safe in my bed upstairs.

But the crowd of visitors in the room, their faces turned expectantly toward my mother, did not belong in the normal morning picture. This was no dream.

My parents began to tell their story, taking turns and interrupting each other from time to time. They told about their anxious wait in the Gestapo yard, their difficult journey to the camp and their exhaustion and despair when they found themselves separated from each other in the transport barracks of Westerbork.

"And then the miracle happened," my mother said, pausing to take a few sips of her soup.

"I really can't call it anything else — it was so strange. Imagine, the person truly responsible for our escaping that train to Poland early this morning was your friend Eleanor!"

Dear Eleanor! Among her many correspondents was a young friend who had lived at Camp Westerbork ever since she and her family had fled across the Dutch-German frontier just before the war. Along with other long-term camp inmates, Hannah Greiser's parents ran the internal camp administration.

Hannah Greiser knew all about me from Eleanor's frequent letters. When Eleanor learned of my parents' arrest, she assumed I had been taken with them and she wrote to Hannah right away, asking her to do what she could for me. Hannah turned to her parents for help. And so Mrs.

Greiser went looking for me among the new arrivals and found my mother instead.

The Greisers conceived a bold scheme to secure a temporary stay of deportation for my parents. Why not request that I might join my parents so that we could travel to Poland as a united family group? It was a way to gain some time — and the Germans liked to deport family groups "intact." They were likely to approve such a request.

"It's a mad scheme, and we are still not quite sure about it," Mother explained. "We weren't sure we wanted to involve Rosemarie. We hoped she might go into hiding and be spared the hardships. But our new friends convinced us otherwise. They have been watching the preparations in Westerbork and they are quite sure that this isn't just a matter of transporting a few thousand "workers" to the East for forced labor. They think it will involve everybody. They feel Rosemarie won't be safe in any case and it would be worse for her to be sent away alone."

My parents' petition was approved at the last moment. Surprisingly, they were both given passes to travel to Amsterdam to bring me back with them. Perhaps the camp commander had been in a good mood that morning.

"It truly is a miracle," Grannie said softly after my mother had finished her story.

"Miracle — coincidence — call it what you will, but here we are!" Daddy said.

"And you are going to stay here now," Mrs. Dubois said firmly. She had slipped into the room after my parents had started to talk and now she came forward to shake hands with them to welcome them home.

"Of course you're not going back," she repeated. "I'll get in touch with some of my friends in the underground right away. We'll find you places to go into hiding — perhaps still tonight."

But my father shook his head.

"Thank you," he said quietly. "It's good to know that we have such wonderful friends, but we can't accept your offer. Remember, we left hostages behind. The Greisers and others vouched for our return. Those people are very much in the clutches of the Germans. I'd hate to think what would happen to them if we didn't return."

Even Mrs. Dubois couldn't argue that point.

After a while, everybody left. It was good to have my parents all to myself.

"I hope we did right, darling," my mother said. "I just pray that we made the right decision about you."

I hugged her fiercely. "Of course, you did," I cried. "I wanted to go with you. I wanted to go the first time."

I rubbed at my eyes, trying to brush away the tears that suddenly blurred my vision.

"Well, you needn't be sorry you missed these last four days," Daddy said, making me smile through my tears.

Later in bed, I couldn't sleep. There were so many things to think about. Eleanor, for example. How strange that Eleanor, who could do so little for herself, had managed to do so much for us. I pictured her sitting ramrod straight at her typewriter, her fingers flashing over the keys, her eyes staring blankly at the wall behind her desk. Odd that I hadn't thought about going to Eleanor during my troubles, but that Eleanor had thought of me. And now it was too late for me to tell her. I would ask Grannie to get in touch with Eleanor tomorrow morning.

Grannie! I felt sick at the thought of Grannie being left all alone. I had asked my parents why Grannie couldn't come with us too. They had explained that it was different for Grannie. Old people might be left alone — they were of little use in a labor camp. Perhaps the war would soon be over — there was still the hope that the Allies might come. With me it was different. Here I was, getting older every day. I'd be fifteen next spring and at sixteen I would be called for labor service.

But that was a year and a half away! Did my parents really expect the war to go on that long?

Parting from Grannie was terribly hard. She had kept busy until the very last, fussing over our breakfast, fiddling with the straps on my rucksack, running the iron over my mother's blouse one last time. When we were all ready to go she ran back to the kitchen once more to bring some hard-boiled eggs she had forgotten to tuck into our lunch box.

The last time there had been no chance to say good-bye. This time Grannie clung to each one of us, postponing the moment of parting.

None of us knew when we would see each other again — if ever.

Halfway down the block we looked back and she was still standing in front of the house, waving. Then a neighbor gently led her inside and closed the door.

I slipped my hand into my father's hand as we walked in silence. It will be all right, I told myself. Everything will be all right, as long as we are together.

Westerbork

August 1942-January 1944

Chapter 6

WE WERE SILENT during the long train ride to the camp. I stared out of the window as we sped through the neat flat countryside, saying good-bye to the checkerboard fields and the sleek brown cows grazing contentedly, to the occasional windmills and the straight, willow-lined canals glistening in the sunlight. I tried to etch these sights on my memory, because Westerbork was so close to the German frontier. When we left there we would be out of Holland and into Germany in a matter of minutes.

It was late in the afternoon when we arrived in Hooghalen, the small railroad station nearest the camp. From there we walked through flat fields and patches of peat bog.

"Look, there it is," my mother said at last. And then I saw the camp, still far in the distance: a jumble of low buildings and fenceposts strung with barbed wire, and tall, rickety wooden guard towers surrounding the whole complex at measured intervals. As we got closer, I could make out the rows of wooden sheds more clearly, their sheet-metal roofs glistening pink in the setting sun.

An SS guard with a tommy gun scrutinized our travel papers before swinging the big gate open to let us in. Then, with a bang and a rattling of chains, he barred it behind us. The sound startled me. There was something so final about it. I looked behind me and saw the gate and fence again and through the strands of wire I saw the open fields and the road along which we had come. But now the fields and the road were outside the gate and I was inside.

The sight gave me an odd, hollow feeling. All day long I had been so happy and relieved that my parents were with me again that I hadn't really given much thought to where we were going and what it would be like. But now it struck me. This was a prison. A prison camp. I had come on my own, without being arrested or having policemen guard me, but I had entered a prison just the same.

Suddenly I was frightened. I reached for my father's hand. He gave me a reassuring smile.

"Here is the registration division," he said. "We must report back here and have you registered."

I clung to him as we entered one of the large wooden sheds, and I kept close to him all through the brief registration procedure. All the while my eyes strayed around the huge, bare room which was set up with long trestle tables to handle the arrival of hundreds of people at one time. Now it was dark and empty except for us and a handful of camp officials shuffling papers at their desks.

Some of the people came to greet my parents. I gathered from the talk that they were the new friends who had helped my parents get passes to Amsterdam.

"Good news," one young man told my father. "We got a further extension for you. At least one transport — possibly two. In any case, you won't have to leave next Tuesday."

I only half listened to the conversation. I didn't really care one way or another whether we stayed or went. As long as I remained with my parents, I didn't care where we were.

My mother put her arm around me.

"Let's go, Rosemarie," she said. "We've been assigned to barracks 43C. That's one of the barracks for people with deferments. I was in a transit barrack before."

One of the women in registration guided my mother and me to our assigned quarters. My father was led away in the opposite direction. We walked past rows and rows of the shedlike buildings, just dim, bulky shapes now that the sun had set. I'd never find my way back to the gate, I thought, as we twisted and turned deep into the center of the camp.

"Here we are," our guide said, opening a door and leading us into a dimly lit room. My first impression was of faces — a lot of pale faces, staring at me. Then the room came into focus and I was aware of beds, too many beds, filling the small space. The three iron double-decker bunks left only a small square of floor space open in the middle of the room. The women were on the beds, some sitting, some lying down. Behind them, another door led into an even smaller room in the back.

"You'll be in there," our friend from registration said. She led us through the front room, helping to maneuver my rucksack and bedroll through the narrow aisle.

The back room too was almost entirely filled by the pair of bunk beds flanking a narrow window. A woman was sitting on the edge of one lower bunk. A girl, not much older than I, was stretched out on her stomach on the bunk above her. When we entered, she sat up and grinned.

"Welcome to the Taj Mahal," she said.

"Hello," the woman said. "I'm Alice Schoenheim. And this is my daughter Ruthie."

While my mother introduced herself and me, I stared at the other beds, which were to be ours. My mother's rucksack and bedroll had been brought over from the transit barracks and placed on the thin, lumpy straw mattress resting on the metal bands of the lower bunk. Mechanically I lifted my own rucksack to the bunk above.

How will I get up? I thought. There's nothing to climb on.

"You'll have to step on the edge of the lower bed and then pull yourself up." Ruthie Schoenheim apparently had guessed my thoughts.

I followed her advice. The coarse mattress

ticking was badly stained and torn, with bits of straw sticking out of the holes. A dark gray army blanket lay folded on one end.

Suddenly I felt terribly tired. All the excitement and anxiety of the last few days and nights seemed to catch up with me. I stared at the ugly spots in the mattress and I knew I should cover them up and start making my bed. But my arms wouldn't obey me. I was unable to move or think or do anything. I just wanted to lie down and cry.

Then my mother was on the bed beside me, spreading the blankets, smoothing them down. Mechanically I helped her, following her motions, pushing or pulling where she told me to pull. I wondered how she still had the strength to keep going.

"This barracks is so much better than the transit barracks where I was first," my mother said. "But I know, to you it must look awful. What you need is a good night's sleep. We both do."

I began to undress, uncomfortably aware of the presence of so many other people. Some of the front-room women had crowded into our room and they were chatting with my mother and Mrs. Schoenheim, completely unaware of me, it seemed. Would I ever adjust to life in a goldfish bowl? I wasn't sure.

"Privacy doesn't come with the accommodations," Ruthie said. This was the second time tonight that she had read my mind. It was uncanny. She was sitting on the bed across from me, setting her hair. She had a little mirror propped up against the wall, and she was calmly winding strand after strand of her brown hair into neat rows of pincurls.

Setting her hair! Why would anyone bother to curl her hair in a prison camp?

Ruthie noticed me watching her and she smiled.

"I've got to hurry," she said. "Lights go out with the curfew whistle at ten. Then it's bedtime for all."

What kind of girl was Ruthie? I wondered. Was she someone I would like? I had a feeling she was laughing at me in a sort of mocking, good humored way.

I shrugged off the question. It really didn't matter, did it? I wouldn't be here long enough to find out.

But as it turned out, we stayed and stayed. Good friends, both inside and outside the camp, were working diligently to keep our names off the transport lists. Each week we packed and unpacked, never quite sure until the last moment whether or not we would have to go.

All through that period I remained in an "I don't care" mood. While my parents were busy adjusting to Westerbork, learning the ropes, getting to know people, I moped around on my bunk or wandered aimlessly among the barracks. What good was it to get to know this camp, I asked myself, if we were not going to stay here anyway? I'd only have to get used to a new place again.

Of course I couldn't avoid getting to know the

people in my barracks. I got to know them far too well. When you were living that closely on top of each other you got to know things about people you didn't want to know. Intimate details about how they washed or chewed their food and what kind of underclothes they wore. We dodged around each other among the unyielding bedframes, stepping over legs and feet and sometimes on each other's toes. All those arms and legs and thighs — all those solid bodies moving and blocking my way and smothering me with their presence. I shrank from the touch of these strangers, wishing they would all vanish by some feat of magic, yearning for just one moment of being alone. Even at night there was never total silence. You could always hear someone breathing or rustling about.

After a while I became resigned to this communal type of living. At least outwardly I did, learning to tuck my things away under my mattress and to wait my turn at the one small sink. As Mrs. Schoenheim kept saying, it was all a matter of good manners and courtesy.

But inside of me, the resentments bubbled. Good manners made me choke down my words when I felt like screaming at the other women. At times I held my hands over my ears to blot out their constant chatter. And when I felt like throwing things around in a fit of rage, I gritted my teeth and dug my fingernails into my palms instead. Oh God, if I would only never have to listen to that thin Miss Hartung's nonstop stories about life in Hamburg again. Or if I could only once get to the sink before bedtime without having to wait for Mrs. Schulberg to finish rinsing out her underwear!

Whenever I felt like that I retreated to my bunk and got out my notebook or the sketchbook I had brought from Amsterdam. I had always been able to shut out the world when I was drawing or writing something.

My mother was unhappy to see me withdraw into myself like that.

"You should try to find some young people," she told me. "It's not good for you to be alone like that all the time. Why don't you try to make friends with Ruthie? She's close to your age. And she always tries to be nice to you."

How could I explain to my mother why I hadn't responded to Ruthie's friendly overtures when I didn't quite understand it myself? It was part of my rejection of everything here in the camp, my not wanting to get involved or attached to something so transient. But partly it was also something about Ruthie herself — her self-assured ways, I suppose, and her slightly disconcerting sense of humor. Ruthie was so different from the girls I had known — different from Anneke and certainly different from me. And the scant year she was older than I couldn't account for that.

Ruthie was fifteen but she seemed a lot older to me. Where I was shy and timid, Ruthie was bold and self-possessed. She had a sharp wit and an uncanny sense of mimicry which she applied mercilessly to the foibles of those around her. It was fun to listen to her, although it was a little unsettling too. But Ruthie was the darling of the barracks. All the elderly ladies in the front room adored her. That beguiling smile and those trusting blue eyes in a heart-shaped face were hard to resist. When it came to begging or borrowing something, Ruthie excelled. It was she who had somehow "organized" the two chairs in our room and the material out of which we had made blackout curtains. "To organize" in camp parlance meant to appropriate and Ruthie was a master in the art.

I don't think Ruthie cared much one way or another how I responded to her. She talked to me, she teased me a little, but when I withdrew she left me alone. She had enough friends of her own.

But the front-room ladies thought I was very standoffish. They kept nagging me to make friends with her. Such a shame, they kept mumbling, two young girls in the same room, and one of them so strange and keeping to herself.

The more everybody nagged me, the more stubborn I got. What did they know? I thought angrily. It's not Ruthie. It's nothing personal. I just don't want to make friends with anyone — not while the war is on — not while everything is so uncertain. I didn't want to lose another friend. There had been Anneke, and Eleanor, and even Julie. And nothing had lasted, nothing was permanent. I wouldn't do it again. I wouldn't fall into that trap.

Chapter 7

WE HAD BEEN in Westerbork several weeks when both of my parents were given responsible camp jobs. My mother was made assistant barracks leader in one of the new transit barracks. My father was given a desk job in the administration. The camp was still growing so rapidly — with more and more huge barracks being built all the time — that the camp staff had to increase too. A job deferment wasn't as good as some of the official deferments, but it was better than nothing at all. At least now we didn't have to worry every single week.

There were all kinds of reasons for people to stay behind in Westerbork. Ruthie's father, for example, was able to stay because he had fought with the German army in the 1914 war and had won the Iron Cross, one of the highest German army decorations. There were several Iron Cross wives and widows in our barracks. Some of the other women felt secure because they had Palestine entry certificates issued by the British government. For some reason the Germans had decided to give preferential status to these people for now.

Then there were the "South Americans." Several Latin American countries had issued "rescue passports" to people hardly able to locate Paraguay, Uruguay, or Costa Rica on a map. The Germans were aware of this fact too, but for the moment the "South Americans" remained protected.

"I'll have to try to write to Lisa about this," my mother said when she heard about the passports. "Lisa might be able to find how one goes about getting passports like that."

Lisa was a cousin who was married to a Swiss. She was marooned in Amsterdam for the moment while her husband tried to arrange for her return with him to Switzerland.

My mother did manage to smuggle a letter out to Lisa and in time Lisa wrote back, indicating guardedly that she had received the message and that she would see what she could do. Shortly afterwards we learned that Lisa had been permitted to return to Switzerland. And that's where the matter rested.

"Lisa will do something," my mother said confidently. But in the meantime my parents had their jobs. "A bird in hand," as my father said.

"Now they'll make you go to work too,"

Ruthie told me. "Everybody over fourteen who stays here for a while is put to work. If you aren't careful they'll stick you in the kitchen to peel potatoes all day long. I think I can help you get a messenger job, like mine. That's much more fun."

A job as a messenger! How I had envied Ruthie's privileged status as a barracks messenger. With her official armband and her pass, Ruthie could go wherever she wanted in the camp. Messengers were very important. Each barracks and each office in the camp had to have one. In a telephoneless society like Westerbork you couldn't do without messengers.

I got the job, and suddenly my life was different. I had things to do and places to go. Now, as I walked around on my errands, the long, low, wooden buildings no longer all looked the same. I began to recognize landmarks within the sprawling barracks complex and the dusty camp roads became purposeful thoroughfares leading to the hospital or the registration unit or to other specific places. And every day I learned more about that strange, self-contained community called Westerbork.

It was a place full of workshops and warehouses, clinics and hospital wards, labs and offices where people filed papers in triplicate. And it was all run by the Jewish inmates of the camp. Except for the guards outside the gate or in the guard towers, I saw fewer Germans in Westerbork than on the streets in Amsterdam. The Gestapo officers were in charge during the weekly loading of the trains to Poland, of course, but the hard fact was that as long as enough passengers reported for deportation each Tuesday morning, the rest of the camp was left to its own devices. In some ways we were freer to talk and act in Westerbork than we had been outside the camp.

In fact, there were some places in Westerbork where you could forget for a few minutes that you were in a prison camp. Or pretend you did. Among the neat barracks quadrangles of the "old camp," for example, where families still lived together in the two-room units built originally by the Dutch government to house refugees. Here there were curtains at the windows and flowerpots before some of the doors, small homey touches that made you think of the world outside.

The Greisers, who had helped to reunite me with my parents, lived in one of those camp apartments. Whenever I had a chance I would impose on their hospitality to relax for a few minutes in their cozy living room. Imagine, the luxury of covered couches, a real table, an easy chair!

"Don't forget, we had to live here since before the war, when all of you were still comfortably in your own homes," Miriam Greiser said defensively when I marveled at all that luxury. "I think we've earned a little bit of privilege."

It was hard to believe that the Greiser's two neat rooms were of the same size and layout as my own quarters in barracks 43C. What a difference some furniture and fewer people could make!

Still, the difference was even greater between 43C and the huge transit barracks where I worked. These large, rough sheds were still being built and filled with rows and rows of triple-decker bunks. The communal washroom, with its rows of sinks and dirty toilets, was at one end of the barracks. The barracks "office," where the staff doled out the food and did the paper work, was at the other. All week long, as transports with prisoners arrived from Amsterdam, batches of new people were brought to the transit barracks. They arrived exhausted, bewildered, in fear. Babies, left for days in the same sodden diapers, howled their discomfort. Toddlers cried with hunger and fatigue. Old people huddled in despair, their belongings lost, their documents in disarray. Many of the newcomers hadn't slept for days, having been kept in the prison pens of the Gestapo. Others had been torn from their beds so hurriedly that they arrived in their nightclothes, with just a coat thrown over their shoulders.

Then came the endless registration procedure in Westerbork. My own arrival had been quick and simple. But the prisoners that arrived in groups spent hours in registration. It took so long to answer all the questions, to fill out all the forms. Then the rough, physical search by Dutch Nazi officials for the last remaining bits of money and jewelry. Finally the shock of their first look at the ugly, dirty barracks where they would spend their last few days on Dutch soil.

It was the job of the barracks staff to make the deportees as comfortable as possible during their brief stay. For me this meant running innumerable errands and escorting people around camp all day long. Those without baggage had to be taken to the welfare warehouse where they could find all kinds of used clothing and blankets and shoes. The sick had to be escorted to various medical and dental clinics. Anxious wives wanted to look for their husbands. Some people wanted to go to the administration barracks to file last-minute appeals for a deferment stamp.

Then Monday came and the tensions mounted. Monday night was transport night. Now was the last possible chance for a deferment — the last chance to do anything.

I rushed around, helping with last-minute packing, soothing babies, doling out bread. Sometimes an errand would send me out just when the long string of cattle cars rumbled onto the tracks that bisected Westerbork like an ugly black slash. There they would stay, casting their threatening shadows across the camp, a silent reminder of why we were all here.

Those cars had been back and forth to those mysterious Polish camps. I didn't really want to look at them, to think about them, but like a magnet they attracted me — made me stop and watch and wonder.

The workmen were scrubbing out the cars, spreading the floors with fresh straw, filling the barrels with drinking water. What had gone on inside those dark, dank windowless boxes on the long journeys east? The stench that wafted across the tracks toward me told part of the story — a foul blending of sweat and vomit and urine and human excrement. The stench would cling to the wooden boards until they rotted away, and no amount of scrubbing would ever rub it out.

CAPACITY: 8 HORSES OR 40 PEOPLE read the legend stenciled on the doors of the cars. But the cars would hold more than twice that number when they left Westerbork early on transport morning. Twice that number and one barrel of water and a second, empty one for sanitary purposes. And nobody knew how long they'd have to be on that train.

I shuddered as I remembered that the people in my transport barracks would have to enter those stinking boxes in the morning. How lucky that they didn't know what lay before them! Most of them hadn't been in Westerbork long enough to see a train or to fully grasp the horror of their impending journey.

I fled, trying to blot the sights and smells from my memory. And when Mrs. Weiss, the barracks leader, sent me home to my own barracks at curfew time, I was glad to go. I didn't want to be with the rest of the barracks staff when they had to awaken their charges before dawn for a last meal of gruel and bread. I didn't want to see them leave the barracks, to lead them through the sleeping camp to the waiting train.

"You go home and get some sleep," Mrs. Weiss usually told me. "We need somebody around here tomorrow morning who is awake enough to help clean up."

Those were her words, but I could read between her lines and I knew what she really meant was: You are young, you need to be shielded, you don't have to see the full horror of what happens on transport nights.

For once I was content to be still a child, to have an excuse for evading the grim realities. It was grim enough in my own barracks on transport nights. On Monday nights there was little laughter in Westerbork. In the gloomy silence there was plenty of time to think about the people I had gotten to know during the past few days who would not be there tomorrow morning. Plenty of time to think and to weep. My arms could still feel the weight of the gurgling baby boy I had played with and cuddled that morning. Where was he now? Had his mother found a bit of straw for him to sleep on? And the brave old lady on crutches I had escorted to the clinic only yesterday afternoon. Had she found a corner in which to sit? How were they all managing inside one of those dark smelly boxes without space to move around, to lie down, to change a baby's diapers? Each time I got that far my mind refused to go on. By shutting out the worst details I was able to bear it.

Gradually, however, my tears came less readily. I stopped looking at the succession of women occupying the barracks beds and they became faceless numbers — just another group to be fed and counted and supplied.

How heartless we are getting, I thought one Tuesday morning as I helped Mrs. Weiss straighten out blankets and mattresses in the still-littered barracks. The thought saddened me, and without quite being aware of doing so, I repeated it aloud.

Mrs. Weiss put down the blanket she was folding and turned around.

"That's self-protection, Rosie," she said. "Pity is a strong emotion, one can take only so much of it. Getting hardened to conditions is nature's way of protecting our sanity. It's like a turtle withdrawing into his shell. Inside he is still just as soft and vulnerable as before."

Mechanically I followed Mrs. Weiss on her rounds — folding blankets, picking up items of discarded clothing, checking toilets and sinks. On Tuesday the transit barracks was always empty except for a few lucky people who had been able to stay behind.

We're in the shipping business, I thought, a terribly efficient, well-run business concerned with the orderly processing and transfer of a product from Holland to points east. Except that our product happens to be people — ordinary people of all ages, sizes, and shapes.

And those people hurrying past me were cogs in this efficient, well-oiled business operation. They ran the kitchens and the hospital, the power plant and the mortuary. Without them the industry of Westerbork could not function.

Why were we doing it? I wondered. What would happen if we all refused to run Westerbork? Perhaps things wouldn't be quite so efficient then.

But when I posed that question to my mother in the evening, she shook her head.

"Would you rather have the Gestapo running the camp?" she asked. "It's bad enough having the SS men with their bayonets at the gate and in the guard towers, and at the train on transport night. Would you rather have them in the barracks and hurling abuse at us all day long? Anyway, if we refused to work, they would send us away and other people would take our places. It's a question of survival, nothing more and nothing less."

I was still troubled. "It sounds wrong," I said.

My mother threw up her hands in mock despair.

"Oh, Rosie, Rosie, when are you going to grow up and face reality? Such an ostrich! Hiding your head in the sand. Sometimes this place reminds me of a jungle and to survive in a jungle you have to fight tooth and claw. As long as you don't go out of your way to hurt someone else. That is important."

"You make me feel as if I were in a zoo," I muttered. "You call me an ostrich and Mrs. Weiss called me a turtle today. I don't want to be an animal in a jungle. I want to be a human being who cares."

I wanted to care, but as Mrs. Weiss had warned me, something inside blunted the things I felt. It was the same with my fears about losing our deferment. Fear somehow couldn't be sustained on a high, insistent pitch. After a while that fear became just part of the daily landscape, something to carry along in the back of one's mind.

I lived my todays. In Westerbork one didn't much like to think of tomorrow.

As the days went on, my attitude toward Westerbork changed. Now when I saw the fences that encircled us, I no longer only thought: That's where our world ends. The fences acquired a new and different meaning. As long as I stayed within their embrace I was safe.

Along with everybody else in camp, I soon wanted desperately to stay in Westerbork.

Chapter 8

IT WAS TRANSPORT Monday again and this time I had to work all night. One of the assistant barracks leaders was sick and the staff was short-handed. Mrs. Weiss asked me to stay.

I had mixed feelings about witnessing a transport for the first time. In a way I felt important and responsible and grown-up. Yet at the same time I wanted to run away, to hide, to be young and ignorant and shielded a little longer. But there was no escape. Tonight I would see the things that, until now, I hadn't wanted even to imagine.

That evening, after curfew, I sat with the rest of the barracks staff sipping hot ersatz coffee and waiting for the hour when we had to awaken the deportees.

The door of the office was half open to the

barracks. Somewhere, far away, a baby was crying. People were coughing, snoring, talking softly, rustling about. Shuffling feet endlessly paced the long center aisle leading to the washroom far off at the other end. Even with my back to the door the ugliness of those rows of triple-decker bunks filled my mind's eye — endless row after row. And the dim lights, burning all night in their shadeless ceiling fixtures.

I must have fallen asleep there in my chair, over my coffee mug, in spite of the low conversations of my fellow workers and the barracks noises seeping in through the door. I woke up to the louder noises of people getting up and getting dressed.

"It's time to serve breakfast and the bread rations," Mrs. Weiss said. "Walk through the barracks, Rosemarie, and see if everyone is awake."

I walked down the aisle, stopping here or there to help buckle a strap or hold a suitcase lid down. One young mother was struggling to quiet her two unruly little girls who were crying on the bed. All three of them wore tightly fitting white cotton turbans on their heads — turbans that covered all of their hair and came way down to the eyebrows, so that their faces seemed strangely naked and wide-eyed below.

It was the standard treatment for hair lice in the camp: the hair cut very short and treated with a strong disinfectant. The acrid lysol fumes wafted across the aisle and stung my eyes.

By the time I returned to the office, people were lining up with enameled mugs and bowls for their last meal in Westerbork. They moved like robots, their faces haggard with fatigue, their eyes dull. Now nothing could save them from the train and the whole barracks was permeated with a feeling of numb acceptance.

Then it was time to leave. The women began to move out of the barracks — a slow, long procession down to the train. Other lines moved out of other barracks, the men and women finally meeting near the train.

With Mrs. Weiss I walked past all the beds to look for luggage left behind. On one bed we found a small cosmetic case filled with medicines.

"That belongs to that gray-haired lady I took to the clinic yesterday," I said. She had reminded me a little of Grannie and I had tried to be specially nice to her.

"Run after her, Rosie," Mrs. Weiss said. "She probably will be lost without these. Try to catch up with her — she won't have reached the checkpoint yet."

I ran through the darkness, past the long lines of people inching their way along. Halfway down to the checkpoint I caught up with my old lady and handed her the little medicine kit, earning a tremulous kiss on my cheek in return.

From here the road sloped down a little toward the train and I could see the platform below me. The train loomed enormous in the shadows. Before it the platform was a milling mass of people.

The babble of hundreds of voices blended into a throbbing din, punctuated now and then by a baby's cry, a name being shouted, the hysterical, wordless screams of a woman suddenly pushed beyond endurance by her fate.

One boxcar was just being loaded — hands clutching gratefully at proffered help up the steep step. The searchlights glowed harshly on those clustered inside the still-open doorways. Standing closely packed, their faces an unearthly white in the bright glare, they seemed to be of another world. More white faces peered through the narrow, wire-draped slits in the sides of the cars.

Dozens of German guards stood stiffly, legs apart, bayonets fixed. A woman clawed her way frantically through the crowd on the platform, blindly shoving aside people, dodging around guards. What was she searching for? A child? A husband? Her belongings? I never learned. A guard grabbed her by the arm and shoved her into an open doorway.

Two camp porters pushed past me, carrying a woman on a stretcher. They moved through the crowd, depositing their burden in the next car being loaded. Hands reached out to help the woman inside.

I saw the tall figure of the Kommandant himself, moving through the crowd, imposing in his tall boots and riding breeches, a club in one hand, a huge dog on a leash in the other. People shrank away from him as he passed, but he prodded them with his club, exhorting them to move faster.

My cheeks were wet with tears and my nails dug deep into my palms. Why did I stand there, watching it all? Why didn't I run away, back to the barracks, where I belonged? I didn't want to look, but I couldn't look away.

I wanted to scream and yell — to cry out my anguish like the hysterical woman whose voice was now stilled — to throw myself at the people still streaming down the path to the train.

Stop! Run away! I wanted to tell them. Don't climb into those boxes like a herd of obedient sheep.

But instead I watched the guards closing the sliding doors, one after another, fastening them with their big metal pins. Now the people inside were in darkness. Only those small slits were open to let in light and air for their long journey.

I opened my mouth to cry out my horror and outrage and fury, but, as in a nightmare, all that emerged was a strangled, whimpering moan. Fear had me by the throat and stilled my voice. My hands beat helplessly against the rough boards of the wooden barrier against which I was leaning. The splinters tore at my flesh and the sharp pain shocked me back to the scene before my eyes.

Suddenly I couldn't bear to see anymore. The truth was too much. The truth about those labor camps — about "resettlement" in the east. Had I really ever believed that resettlement in Poland might be no worse than Westerbork? How could anything but horror lie at the end of a journey that started like this?

In a wild frenzy I tore back to the barracks, sucking the blood off my scratched, bleeding hands, choking back my sobs. Why? Why? I kept thinking. Why were we being punished? Why did we have to submit?

Why were we treated like criminals — no, worse, like cattle? Cattle being led to slaughter? But even cattle were transported more gently than this.

Everywhere else prisons and concentration camps were for people who had committed crimes, for saboteurs, for people who threatened the legal government. If you didn't commit crimes, if you were politically passive, you were all right, nothing could happen to you. But that wasn't true for us — it wasn't true for Jews. What was our crime? To have been born? To exist? How could you escape punishment if that in itself was a crime?

Back at the barracks Mrs. Weiss read the anguish in my eyes and sent me home.

"Go to sleep, Rosie, and forget the sights," she said. "In time you will even get used to transport nights."

But I couldn't erase that scene at the train from my mind. Days later I went to visit the Greisers, hoping to forget even for a moment about barracks and ugly sights.

The Greiser girls understood how I felt and tried to cheer me up. Hannah Greiser was two years older than I, Miriam was a year younger. They had been in Westerbork almost three years and between them they knew all the young people in the "old camp." It was a tight little clique, suspicious of strangers.

But Hannah thought that her friends would accept me. She had offered several times to take me along to one of their Youth Group meetings. Hannah and Miriam and all their friends were ardent Zionists. They spent most of their free time studying and talking about Palestine. They were surprised at my nearly total ignorance about it.

"You should learn about Zionism," Miriam told me again. "Lewis will explain it all to you. He is the one who organized the group and taught us all we know. Nobody can explain it the way Lewis can."

Until now I had always refused. I hadn't wanted to join any groups, to make new friendships, to get involved. But now I thought, why not? I had to stop thinking about the trains. Perhaps the Youth Group would give me something new to think about.

So I went to the next meeting. It was held in a small square building that, until recently, had been used as a school room. The Youth Group members sat on benches in a semicircle, listening intently to a slight young man who sat in front of the room, leading the discussion.

Lewis seemed rather ordinary — short and sandy-haired, with a narrow face and sallow complexion. But he had the most intensely blue eyes I had ever seen, eyes that could burn with fervor or soften with compassion. They were the eyes of a visionary, a reformer — and with them he cast a spell on his entire audience.

To me, the meeting was a revelation. These young Jews, I discovered, were proud of their heritage. They did not regard being Jewish as a tremendous burden. They knew as much about the great Jewish heroes of five thousand years ago as most people knew about contemporary leaders. And they looked to these heroes as models for a new Jewish state. Under the shadows of the prison fences, with deportation to Poland hanging over their heads, they worked and studied feverishly to prepare themselves for a possible future in a Palestine kibbutz.

I'd never met young people like these. Perhaps there had been some in my Jewish school in Amsterdam but I hadn't known any of them. Now, at this meeting, the talk filled me with excitement. Perhaps I too might learn to be proud and to find meaning in my heritage.

At the end of the session, Hannah introduced me to Lewis. It didn't take him long to recognize my complete ignorance of all things Jewish. And he had little patience with such a state of affairs.

"My God, it's a crime, letting you grow to this age without teaching you anything about the history that shaped our present dilemma," he said angrily. "How can you be strong and proud if you weren't given anything to be proud about? If you have to suffer through this insanity, you ought at least to know what it is all about!"

I didn't quite understand his outburst — I just had a sinking feeling that Lewis had rejected me. But then I noticed that his eyes had softened at the edges.

"Well?" he asked gruffly. "Do you want to learn? It will mean working very hard to catch up. You'll need to know Iwrit — the modern Hebrew — to prepare for life in Palestine. I'll teach you in my spare time, if you like. And I'll lend you books on Jewish history."

Would I like to? Of course I would! I'd have studied Chinese or Hindi if that were a requirement to become part of the group. Here was something to believe in — a ray of hope — something new and exciting to think about. And an hour ago I hadn't even been sure that I wanted to come to the meeting!

"Gee, you are lucky," Miriam whispered when we hurried out of the meeting room just before curfew time. "Most of us would give our eye-teeth to have private lessons from Lewis. Imagine, spending a whole hour with him alone!"

"I guess sometimes it pays to be ignorant," I said happily, caught up in her mood. There was something magical about Lewis. I couldn't remember when I had last felt quite this carefree and relaxed.

After that, my life revolved around the Youth Group and around my studies with Lewis. In the evening, after working hours, I'd meet Lewis somewhere — in the empty schoolroom or sometimes even in the "old camp" room he shared with two other young men. He had a treasure trove of books that he had brought with him when he had fled to Holland from Germany before the war, and we'd pore over those books, delving into Jewish history.

The rest of my daily routine receded into the background. I knew that my parents were still struggling and scheming for more permanent protection, for a solid deferment that would keep our names off the transport lists. Their fatigue and strain and worry showed in their faces, but they didn't burden me with details and I really didn't want to know.

Ruthie made fun of my newly found interest in Zionism. Girl Scout stuff, she called it. And she thought that the Youth Group was just ridiculous. A bunch of kids sitting around and finding nothing better to talk about than Jewish history. Ruthie had no use for groups like that. She never had any trouble, either, finding company for herself when she wanted to be with other people.

I ignored Ruthie's gibes about the Youth Group.

With Lewis I began to explore some of the questions that had haunted me ever since the Germans had marched into Holland and had wrecked our happy life.

Why were these things happening, I asked him — why to me, why to the Jews? As we delved deeper into Jewish history, there were some answers — a pattern of repeated persecutions, a continuity of suffering running throughout the centuries. It still didn't make sense, had never made sense, in whatever century it had happened. But here we were, caught up in one of these periodic waves of madness, only it was worse this time, much worse because this time there was no escape. And now it was happening to people I knew, people I loved, and to me!

"And that's why we *must* have a Jewish state," Lewis told me when I asked questions. "A place where we can feel safe. This is what

Zionism is all about. We must never let anything like this happen again."

Yes, what he said was right, I knew. And yet, deep down, I still longed to return to my old life. I didn't really yearn for a still-unborn state thousands of miles away, but for Amsterdam, just a scant ninety miles beyond the horizon. But I let the fervor of the others sweep me along. With them I sang "L'Shanah Haba'ah B'Yerushalayim" ("Next Year in Jerusalem") and I learned to dance the Hora, the exuberant Jewish circle dance. At first I felt timid about joining the tight circle of dancers and my feet were awkward at the unfamiliar steps. But the wild, joyous sound of the music made my heart beat faster in rhythm to the beat and I finally abandoned myself to the joy of being spun around in a circle of friends.

Summer slipped into fall almost unnoticed. In the treeless camp, the change of seasons could be observed only through the changes in the weather: There were no autumn leaves to herald winter's coming, no store windows displaying winter coats, no school terms to measure the passage of time.

I had never studied so hard in school as I worked now to perfect my mastery of the unfamiliar Hebrew letters. I wanted desperately to learn enough to become a full-fledged member of the Youth Group. I still remained an observer only because I didn't know enough to be able to join the spirited discussions. I worked hard because I wanted to please Lewis. When Lewis praised me, I felt my cheeks flush and later I'd awaken thinking of just how he had been pleased. How he had looked. His words. But there were times when he was critical too. At first I took his words and said nothing but gradually I gained in confidence.

"It isn't possible that you don't know this," he snapped at me one day when I couldn't answer one of his questions. "My God, I was taught these things before I was six or seven. Wasn't there any religion in your home?"

For once I felt stung to defend myself.

"My parents taught me that one doesn't need the ritual of a religious service to reach God," I flung back. "I believe in God, and my parents do too, but I don't see much sense in lots of the rules and rigmarole set up by man."

"Neither do I," Lewis said, surprisingly. "But I feel a certain satisfaction in continuing a tradition set up nearly five thousand years ago. The rules and regulations were the cement that held the Jews together and preserved their identity during the centuries of exile. And they will be needed again, as a framework for building a Jewish state, for it will be a state that has grown out of a religion."

"And look where all that identity has got us," I argued. "Perhaps it would have been better if that cement had not been so strong. A lot of people might have been spared a great deal of persecution. Just think of the Inquisition alone!"

"Well, a lot of Jews did abandon their faith during the Spanish Inquisition," Lewis said quietly. "Do you think you might have chosen that way?"

"Yes, I think I might," I admitted. "I might now too, if the Germans would let us. But the Nüremberg laws put the Inquisition to shame. Remember that group of priests and nuns with the yellow stars being sent off to Poland two weeks ago? Hitler won't even let us abandon a faith we were born into if we are willing to!"

I gave Lewis a sidelong glance, wondering how he would take my outburst. Stupid, I told myself. Why did I have to be so honest? Perhaps Lewis will despise me now.

But Lewis only laughed. "I guess I've got my work cut out for me as a teacher — because it's up to the teacher to convince his students of his point of view. I'd better lend you some more books to acquaint you with your ancestry."

I wondered whether my relief showed in my face. I watched silently as Lewis selected a half dozen volumes from the tall stack of books piled up on the floor next to his bed. When he turned back to me, his original anger had evaporated and he relented a bit.

"You've really done remarkably well so far, Rosemarie," he told me. "I shouldn't be so hard on you. In fact, I feel you are ready to take part in our Chanukah play next month. You could be one of the candle lighters. It will mean memorizing some Hebrew lines, but you should be able to do it. We'll be assigning parts at the next meeting anyway."

My arms filled with books, I walked home through the brisk November air, my mind awhirl. Lewis was great, kind, wise, and wonderful! I had never felt so alive, so sure of myself and other people. And in a strange way I had never felt so free and liberated — freed from my own inhibitions and insecurity. It was an odd thing to accomplish in the midst of a prison camp, but then of course the mind was an independent creature, unbound by prison walls.

My mind wandered to the Chanukah play and in spite of the cold wind I felt warm with contentment. Chanukah. The big day was still more than a month away, time enough in which to learn my part and to savor my new role in the Youth Group.

Here I was, letting myself plan ahead beyond tomorrow, allowing myself the luxury of looking forward to a future event. In spite of my resolve, I was tossing caution to the wild November winds.

Chapter 9

I REMAINED IN that rather elated mood all through December. The Chanukah play was a success. Lewis praised me for saying my lines correctly and for the next few days I walked on air. Life could be wonderful — even in Westerbork! I redoubled my efforts at learning Hebrew just to show Lewis how much I cared.

But the new year brought stormy skies and wet snow that turned the camp streets into slushy rivers of mud. Icy winds blew across the peat bogs, driving people into the smelly, noisy barracks to huddle in steamy discomfort. The dampness followed through the chinks around the windows and the cracks under the doors. Everything we touched felt cold and clammy — even the beds where we sought warmth.

The rumors too were depressing. There was

nothing but talk about Allied defeats. The war seemed to be going badly everywhere: at the Russian front, in Italy, in North Africa. People stopped talking about a British invasion. At the moment it seemed more likely that Hitler might make good on his boast that he would conquer England.

It was during those cold, depressing winter months that I began to lean more and more on Ruthie. When everyone else around us walked about with long and gloomy faces, Ruthie still managed to crack a joke and to find something to laugh about. I don't know exactly when our relationship started to change . . . when it was that Ruthie began to take Anneke's place in my life. I guess it happened quite naturally. Suddenly, one day, we were best friends, confiding in each other, sharing secrets and attitudes. And yet it was an odd friendship. We couldn't have been more different in the things we liked to do or talk about.

I suppose if Ruthie and I hadn't shared that one tiny room we would never have become friends. But here we were, two "only children" suddenly living together as closely as only two sisters could. And Ruthie treated me just the way she would have treated a slightly younger sister — sharing her thoughts with me and then going her own way. I, in turn, looked up to Ruthie, and trusted her implicitly. But then, that was the way I had leaned on Anneke too.

Ruthie was popular and I envied her easy-going way with boys. She'd tease them or giggle with them one moment and then walk away arm in arm with one, deep in a serious conversation. I watched her, trying to learn from her, but I wasn't very successful; every time a boy just looked in my direction I instantly turned into a blushing and tongue-tied idiot.

Ruthie tried hard to pull me out of my shell. "Don't be so self-conscious," she scolded. "Boys are shy too and you'll only scare them off if you act so uncomfortable in their company."

She was right, of course, but I couldn't change. I'll never learn how, I decided. Not in a million years. You have to be born that way.

Maybe after the war, I consoled myself. Maybe when things are normal again and I'm back in school with boys around me in class. Perhaps then I'll learn how to behave around them.

"After the war!" Ruthie scoffed. "Why should you wait until then? Who knows how long it will be. I'm fifteen now and I want to do the things you are supposed to do when you are fifteen. Maybe I'll be an old maid by the time the war is over. I'm not going to let Hitler cheat me out of all my teenage fun."

As the winter faded into a bleak spring, Ruthie's long list of admirers dwindled. Suddenly the only name that kept cropping up in our whispered nighttime conversations was Piet. I had seen Piet with Ruthie — a gangling, freckle-faced redhead who had been tagging after her for months, it seemed. But now it was only Piet she talked about and Piet who took her for walks on the heath.

The "heath" was a strip of unused land at one end of the camp behind the last row of mammoth storage barracks. The ground sloped steeply here toward the barbed wire fence so that this bit of land had not been used to build more barracks. The heath was the only spot within the confines of the camp where anything grew besides pale, dusty grass: In the summer and fall the steep rocky slope was covered with a blush of pale purple heather. If you sat on a rock with your back to the barracks, you could gaze out through the barbed wire strands across the rolling heath and toward the dark woods in the distance, and you could pretend that the fence wasn't there.

To us, the heath, small as it was, was a lovers' lane, a picnic ground, a place to feast the eyes. And when you walked hand in hand with a boy on the heath on a Sunday afternoon, it was almost like putting an engagement announcement in the paper. Everybody saw and knew what it meant.

I tried to imagine myself walking on the heath on a Sunday with a boy — a faceless boy, because there just wasn't anybody I could picture in that role.

"What about Lewis?" Ruthie teased. "Why don't you ask your precious Lewis to take you walking on the heath?"

To my dismay I felt myself blushing wildly.

Why did Ruthie have to keep teasing me about Lewis? Didn't she realize that Lewis was unobtainable — that he was simply out of reach. Lewis wasn't just another teenage schoolboy, like Piet or Ruthie's other friends. Lewis was nearly twenty, really grown-up, and beyond a schoolgirl crush like mine. I couldn't even imagine Lewis walking on the heath with one of the older girls, someone closer to his own age. Lewis just wasn't that type. Conceivably he might sit on the heath with me, book in hand, patiently testing my knowledge of Jewish history. But a romantic boy-girl stroll? Never!

Toward the end of March we celebrated Ruthie's birthday. She was sixteen years old and everyone in barracks 43C rallied to make it a special day for her.

Mrs. Schulman, the rotund and cheerful apartment "eldest," miraculously produced a birthday cake. Her camp job was somehow peripherally connected with the camp kitchens, and everyone tactfully refrained from asking how she had come by it. It was a tiny cake, hardly more than a mouthful for everyone, but it somehow supported a tight cluster of seventeen little candles — sixteen pink ones and one white one "to grow on."

"I'm getting too old," Ruthie giggled. "Too many candles to blow out. I don't think I can make it!"

She closed her eyes and she blew and made it.

"Cocoa anyone?" Mrs. Schoenheim asked. In honor of the occasion she had dipped into her precious reserves and had brought forth some cocoa and condensed milk for a rare and unexpected treat.

I sat back, against Mrs. Schulman's lower bunk, my hands cupped around my cocoa mug, slowly sipping the sweet, chocolate brew. Somewhere deep in my mind a memory stirred . . . myself at breakfast back home . . . wasting cupfuls of hot cocoa because a skin had formed and because I really didn't want to drink it anyway. A lifetime ago.

With an effort, I brought myself back to the party. We were crowded into the larger front room of 43C — crowded because besides the ten women sharing the two rooms assorted husbands had been smuggled in to share in the celebration. People sat on the bunks, on the few chairs available, on empty crates and upturned suitcases. With the cocoa we toasted the birthday child.

"Happy birthday, Ruthie! Happy sweet sixteen!"

Ruthie accepted the honors cheerfully. "Thank you, thank you," she said, and then she laughed.

"Sweet sixteen, indeed," she mocked. "This is the year of my emancipation. I'm of age now — Hitler said so — not at thirteen or eighteen or twenty-one, but of age at sixteen.

Everyone knew what she meant. At sixteen, young people were considered independent of their parents — to be deported on their own, no longer sheltered by whatever reprieve their parents still might possess. It was a jarring note, destroying the momentary fiction that this was just a happy birthday party.

Next to me, Mrs. Schoenheim stiffened.

"This isn't quite the sweet sixteen party I had planned for Ruthie," she whispered to my mother. "You are fortunate that Rosemarie will be only fifteen on her birthday next month."

Just moments before, I had envied Ruthie for having reached that momentous, magical milestone of sixteen, but suddenly I felt lucky. I looked at Ruthie, who was sitting crosslegged on the floor examining her birthday gifts – trifling odds and ends people had found among their possessions and wrapped up as gifts for her: a scarf, a pocket comb, a hair ribbon, some apples, and, most magnificently, a Droste chocolate bar. The latter had been a gift from Piet, who recently had been acknowledged as Ruthie's steady boyfriend. He was here now, sharing the moment with her, his long legs folded uncomfortably under him, the first soft shadow of blond down showing on his upper lip and cheeks.

How happy Ruthie looks, I thought. Different too – as if that extra candle on her cake had suddenly pushed her that much closer toward adulthood. She was slipping away from me somehow . . . away toward an age of love and responsibility and thoughts of marriage.

It occurred to me that everyone in the room was in pairs except for me and that tall, thin Miss Hartung. Miss Hartung had been a spinster for God only knew how many years, and presumably she was used to her status. But what about

119

me? Would I grow up to be like Miss Hartung some day?

Back home, in normal times, I probably wouldn't have worried yet about these things. After all, I wasn't quite fifteen — my God, there was lots of time to think about dating and marriage. But here something of Ruthie's urgency had somehow rubbed off on me. It was so hard to know what the future would bring. How could you tell what it was like in those camps in far-off Poland — whether there would be a chance there to meet boys, to learn about love. Maybe the only thing ahead of us were years and years of slave labor . . .

No, I wouldn't permit myself such morbid thoughts. Of course my chance would come one day — the war was bound to end, surely, and the Allies would come to rescue us. It couldn't be long now — the war had been going on for years.

Around me the birthday party was still in full swing. Everyone was laughing and having a good time. I got up and maneuvered myself through the tangle of legs and bodies to the other side of the room where my father was perched on a packing case. Leaning against him, with his arm around me, I suddenly felt snug and warm and secure. I didn't need to worry about boys and grown-up responsibilities — not yet, anyway.

Chapter 10

RUTHIE'S PARTY was the last good thing that happened that spring. At least it seemed that way. It wasn't as if people weren't trying to find something hopeful to talk about. Spring, with its longer days and bright sunshine, brought new hope even to Westerbork. The trouble was that any talk about German losses, about shortages in war supplies or rolling stock, seemed disproved by the persistent weekly departures of the trains. Surely a nation concerned with battlefield defeats and air attacks would have more pressing things to worry about than to clear the occupied countries of whatever Jews still remained.

But the trains kept rolling and new people kept coming from Amsterdam or other cities as fast as the security police could hunt them out and round them up. Where were they all coming from? I wondered. Sometimes it seemed as if the supply of Jews should have dried up long ago. But the Gestapo always managed to find new victims. They were arrested on the streets, picked up at home, flushed out of hiding places. Now the names on the transport lists always seemed to include someone we knew. Few of us still had any friends or relatives left in Amsterdam or other places "outside."

One person who hadn't come yet, however, was Grannie. My mother worried about her all the time, and so did I. Was it really possible that she had escaped the dragnet raids until now? It was a miracle. But her luck surely couldn't last much longer. She was bound to arrive one of these days. And what would we do then?

Every so often at work, when a new batch of people arrived in the transit barracks, I would glimpse a head of white hair and a slight form and my heart would stand still for a moment. Grannie! I'd think, and then the person would turn around and she wouldn't look at all like Grannie.

Could it be that they had forgotten about her? I wondered. She was living alone in that boarding house. There were no other Jews living there at all now. But deep in my heart I knew that I was fooling myself. The Gestapo never forgot anybody.

My mother started to talk about the South American passports again. Lisa had let us know that the passport matter was definitely in the works. It was just a matter of time.

"But we have no time," my mother sighed. "If Grannie comes before the passports, there is nothing I can do to keep her here."

Then one day while I was at work, slicing large loaves of bread into individual rations, my mother burst into the barracks office. I looked at my mother's face and knew that something was wrong.

"Bad news," my mother said quietly. "I've just had the word that Grannie is here. She is passing through registration right now with a large group of mostly elderly people."

And before I could answer she was gone again, so quickly that I wondered if I had dreamed it all. I stood there, with my knife poised in mid-air over the next loaf of bread and all I could think was: Grannie ... Grannie ... Grannie ...

Then Mrs. Weiss came into the office and I went back to work. In Westerbork a lot of people's grandmothers had come and gone. It was nothing remarkable enough to comment about.

I saw Grannie later that evening. She seemed smaller and older than I remembered her. Was it possible that it was less than a year since we had seen her last? The tense, anxious months she had spent all alone in Amsterdam had taken their toll.

My mother had managed to find a bed for Grannie in the old-age barracks next to the hospital compound. It was less crowded than the regular transit barracks and they had double-decker bunks instead of the triple-decker ones.

After her first exhaustion and bewilderment

had worn off, Grannie seemed remarkably self-possessed. At the moment she was happy just to see us again.

"But I won't be able to keep her here," my mother cried later that evening when we were alone. "She won't have to go next Tuesday — the lists for that transport are filled already — but the week after that they are going to make up a special transport of the aged. They are going to empty out the old-age barracks. And there is nothing I can do for Grannie then."

Grannie herself was much more complacent about it all than my parents or I. During the next few days I slipped in to see her whenever I had a moment to spare and I always found her sitting on her bunk with a smile on her face and with her knitting in her hands. I'd curl up on the end of her bed, and we'd talk and talk while Grannie knitted endlessly on new sweaters for me from wool she had unraveled from something old.

It was Grannie who taught me to look on life as an adventure and not to give in to fear. Grannie refused to be afraid.

"At my age, Rosie darling, nothing can really scare you quite as much as when you're young. Even death somehow begins to lose its terror. There are times, in fact, when it seems like a rather attractive alternative, all things considered. After all, I've had a good life, bringing up children, seeing them grow up. . . ."

She paused, her head bent over her knitting as she counted a row of stitches.

"That's the way your grandfather felt," she continued when she looked up again.

"Your grandfather had great strength of will. When the Nazis took over Austria and it looked as if we would have to flee, he just refused to contemplate it. He felt he was too old to start life anew in a foreign country. If they wouldn't let him live the way he liked, he didn't want to live at all. So he took to his bed and he literally willed himself to die. He wasn't really sick but a week later he was dead — he had died in his sleep. It was what he wanted to do."

Grannie's eyes misted over as she remembered. But a moment later she smiled at me.

"Of course, that's not my way," she declared. "There is too much curiosity about life in me to give up on it voluntarily. There are too many interesting things happening every day. New and unexpected things lurking around every corner. Even the bad things that happen are interesting in their way. You just have to pretend that you are looking at them from the outside."

"But how can you?" I cried. "How can you manage to stay so calm when everyone else in camp is half sick with fear and worry? All that uncertainty, all this business about not knowing what lies at the other end of those trains — to me, that's not an adventure, that's more like a nightmare!"

"And would my worrying about it change anything?" Grannie shook her head. "It makes sense to struggle only when you can achieve something by doing so. There are times to act and times to bend with the storm. As for staying calm — that is something you must find within yourself. It's there, you know, inside of every one of us. You just have to learn how to find it. It's a place to hide when the storm tosses around you — like the calm, still eye of the hurricane. Deep in there, the storm cannot touch you."

She reached out and took my hand in hers.

"If I worry at all," she said, "it is you I worry about. It is hard to be young in times like these. The young carry the responsibility for the future on their shoulders. When you're old, you've done your share. It doesn't matter anymore."

She went back to her knitting then and I left, puzzled but yet strangely comforted. At the door I looked back and saw her still hunched over her work on the edge of her cot, a small island of serenity in the midst of the normal barracks hubbub. How long, I wondered, did it take to find that core of peacefulness within oneself? Grannie was past seventy — she'd had a long time to search. But I needed the answer then, not forty or fifty years later.

I suppose I meant to cheer up Grannie and to comfort her during my visits — after all, she was the one who would have to leave. But it didn't quite work out that way. I found myself pouring my heart out to Grannie. My parents were too busy, too harassed, to bother with my little worries. But Grannie seemed to have all the time in the world to listen, to comfort, to advise. Even now, when I knew our days together were numbered, there seemed to be a timeless quality to our talks.

She listened, and then, once in a while, she talked to me. About all kinds of things. She was passing her wisdom on to me, bit by bit, as if she wanted to cram it all into that last brief span of shared time.

We talked again about death. The thought of death seemed to lie close to the surface these days—not often spoken about but never forgotten. In the old-age barracks death was a daily guest. And the unspoken question hung heavy in the air: Would any of the people survive the ordeal before them?

"Don't be afraid of death, Rosie," Grannie told me. "Death is hard on the people who are left behind. But don't pity the dead. Who knows what they find. Peace and oblivion, a release from pain, perhaps even a new adventure—a different form of existence to explore and enjoy."

She fell silent while she attended to her work, unraveling the last few rows she had fashioned while we talked. I watched her undo the stitches, winding the wool neatly back onto the ball.

A different form of existence, I thought, trying to fathom her thought. Like the wool—round like a ball, one way—and then worked neatly into compact rows, a totally different form altogether.

Then Grannie went on talking, without looking at me, as if she hadn't paused at all.

"When my time comes, Rosie, promise me you'll remember that I have always been curious about what lies on the other side. For me, that will be a new adventure."

"But you're not going to die!" I cried, reaching for her hand. "You're not going to, you're not going to. . . ."

Grannie smiled.

"That won't be up to me, will it?" she asked quietly. "There are higher powers . . ."

Did she mean God? Or the Germans? I wasn't quite sure.

Another day we talked about being alone. My friend Julie, from the Jewish school, had passed through Westerbork recently. Found in hiding, she had come without her parents and been sent on by herself.

This could have happened to me, I remembered. What if my parents hadn't come to get me that day in Amsterdam? I might have been found in hiding and been sent to Poland all alone too. The thought of being alone haunted me.

"I know I couldn't stand it," I told Grannie.

"It's hard to be alone," Grannie agreed. "But you'll discover someday that in the long run we are all alone. God willing, you won't have to find out until you're old enough and ready for it." Grannie patted my hand. "I have faith in you, Rosie," she said. "I'm sure you'll be able to cope with anything life brings you."

I hoped that Grannie's trust in me was not misplaced. I wasn't so sure.

And then there was no more time with Grannie because her transport time had arrived. The

128

old-age transport was supposed to go to a camp in Czechoslovakia, not to Poland at all.

"They say Theresienstadt is like a real town — with apartment houses and everything," my mother said the day before Grannie was to leave. "Perhaps it is better than Westerbork."

We clung to the hope. We didn't want to believe that it might not be true.

Once again, it was Grannie who comforted us.

"Don't worry about me," she said. "I managed to take care of myself in Amsterdam — I'll get along now too."

She rummaged in her big carry-all and she pulled out the scarf she had been knitting for me the past couple of days.

"You'll have to finish it yourself, Rosie," she said. "Just another twenty rows or so to go. It will wrap around your neck twice that way."

I reached blindly for the bundle of red and blue wool, trying to hide the tears in my eyes. But Grannie wasn't fooled.

"Don't cry, Rosie," she pleaded. "There is always a time in life when people must part. And when the time has come, it does no good to cry or to lament. If all goes well, we'll be together again when the war is over. Until then, just keep up your courage and make the best of each day."

But this was one parting too many for me. I couldn't bear to think of Grannie on that train, all alone, squeezed into the darkness and stench with a lot of uncaring strangers. Would she even survive the trip? It was hard enough for young strong people. But Grannie!

For my mother's sake I hid my worry and anxiety. She used her official position to accompany Grannie to the train. I don't know how she could bear to stay with Grannie to the very end. I was coward enough not even to ask how the parting had gone. I wanted to pretend that it hadn't really happened.

Chapter 11

AFTERWARDS, we stopped talking about Grannie. My mother even stopped talking about the South American passports. Somehow she didn't seem to care about them anymore.

For the first time in months I turned to my notebook to blot out reality, the things that were happening around me. When my mind was groping to scan a verse I didn't have to think of Grannie.

Ruthie helped too. You never could be glum for a long time around Ruthie. She had a new job now at the camp hospital, running errands for the head doctor there and she always came back full of anecdotes about things that had happened that day. I tagged after her in my free time, happy to let her plan things for both of us to do. Why couldn't I be more like Ruthie?

Life would be so much easier. Ruthie never sat around brooding about things she couldn't change. She was always too busy for that.

But then one day I returned to our room and I found Ruthie stretched out on her bed, just staring at the ceiling. She didn't even seem to hear me come in, for she didn't stir until I called her name. Then she sat up and looked at me, and there was a stunned, disbelieving look on her face.

"I've got to leave on the next transport," she said. "It really happened. They called up a lot of kids my age who aren't under their parents' deferment anymore."

"Oh, Ruthie, no!" I was horror-stricken.

"Something will turn up," I cried. "Someone will help. What about your job! Can't they do something to keep you here? I'm sure they will try!"

The chief doctor was an influential man and I knew he was fond of Ruthie. Surely he would try to help.

Ruthie shook her head.

"I already asked," she said. "There is nothing he can do. This is a group action. I'll have lots of company. Piet was called too."

I thought of Ruthie's birthday party and how flippantly she had predicted her fate. Just a few months ago that was — and now her joking words had turned into a grim truth.

That moment of stunned silence on her bed was the only moment of weakness Ruthie allowed herself. Afterwards she was amazingly calm.

"I won't be alone," she comforted her mother,

who had almost collapsed at the news. "Piet will be going too. I don't mind going as long as we are together. Piet will look after me."

I rather doubted it. Piet was too gentle and shy to act the big protector. More likely it would be Ruthie who would look after both of them. But as long as Piet's presence comforted Ruthie, I certainly did not voice those thoughts.

My mother and I helped Ruthie get ready for her journey since her own mother seemed almost paralyzed with grief. But Ruthie did most of her packing herself. Even now she found things she could joke about. Hers was not the numb, frozen acceptance I had witnessed so often in the transit barracks. Ruthie seemed confident that she would be able to manage her own affairs.

"Don't worry about me," she laughed. "A bad penny always turns up." But when we embraced that last evening, there were tears in her eyes.

Still, too much seriousness went against her nature.

"Remember what I told you about boys, Rosie," she said, trying to smile through her tears. "I want to have good reports from you when we see each other again!"

Westerbork seemed empty after Ruthie's departure. The emptiness was inside of me. It had taken so long to fill the gap Anneke had left in my life. Even the Youth Group couldn't divert my thoughts to more pleasant matters. The group was breaking up too. Reality was reaching into our little make-believe world and claiming victims for the trains.

I'd go to the meetings and pretend to take part in whatever the others were doing, but half of the time I hardly listened. My thoughts were with Grannie or Ruthie or the other friends who had disappeared into the limbo called Poland.

And so I almost missed Lewis' important announcement until everybody else around me gasped and started to protest.

Lewis had just announced that he would volunteer for the next transport. A whole group of his charges was to leave and he had decided to go with them.

"They need me more than those of you who are staying here," he declared. "Perhaps we can start a Youth Group in those Polish camps. We'll get it going and it will be ready for you when the rest of you come."

The rest of us! Now even Lewis didn't doubt that sooner or later everybody would be taken away from Westerbork. And so he was leaving now.

I couldn't believe it. Lewis couldn't desert us! He couldn't really have volunteered for that journey into the unknown. Without Lewis the Youth Group couldn't possibly function. It was his enthusiasm and zeal that had created this center of meaning for us in a meaningless world.

Lewis of course assumed that we would just go on.

"Joshua will take my place as group leader," he told us. "I trust you will work with him as enthusiastically as you did with me. And of course I expect to meet all of you after the war in Jerusalem!"

We crowded around him, shook his hand, echoed his confident "Shalom." But I don't think any of us really shared his belief in a speedy reunion. If we didn't start crying in front of him, it was mostly because we didn't want to let him down.

How often Ruthie had teased me about my feelings for Lewis. Now I looked up for a last time into those commanding blue eyes of his, and suddenly I felt confused. What were my feelings about Lewis? Could Ruthie have been right? Had I loved him without really understanding what I felt?

I stood there, trying to sort my feelings out. How did you know if you were in love? What was it you were supposed to feel? Did I feel about Lewis what Ruthie felt about Piet?

I felt my cheeks flaming at the thought. How awful if I had loved Lewis all along and hadn't realized it until the very night before he was leaving camp!

I wanted to share my thoughts and feelings with someone, but there was no one to share them with. Grannie might have comforted me with wise words. My mother might have hugged me and let me cry, but how could I go to her, grieving as she was now over her own friends who had left on the trains.

Ruthie would have understood. She would have been pleased with me. Oh, if I could only have run home to my barracks to tell Ruthie about it all!

Suddenly, for the first time since my first few weeks in the camp, Westerbork truly became a prison to me. The noise, the smells, the ugliness of the barracks, the harsh pattern of the encircling barbed-wire fencing assailed me. Where had I been all this time that I hadn't been aware of how horrid and depressing Westerbork really was?

"You are growing up, Rosie," my mother said, when I told her. "Until now you had your head buried in the sand. You didn't want to see."

Maybe I was growing up. I was fifteen, after all. I wasn't a child anymore. But it hadn't been sand that had shielded my vision from the truth until now. It had been people — the people around me — friends like Ruthie and Lewis, who had made Westerbork bearable. And now there was nothing between me and the ugly fences.

My parents too went around grim-faced and in silence, each one absorbed by private worries and fears.

And the days crept by. We marked the New Year with thoughts of hope. Perhaps 1944 would be a better year. Perhaps it would bring peace and liberation.

One day my father was summoned to the registration building. A large, official-looking manila envelope had been delivered for him by a courier from Amsterdam. He brought it to my mother and we opened it together. Inside were the South American passports my mother had been praying for all those months.

There were four passports, one for each of us and one for Grannie. But Grannie's had come too late. My mother pushed them aside. She didn't even want to talk about them. Not now that Grannie was gone.

But she wasn't allowed to forget about them for long. Suddenly, early in January, there was a lot of talk about South American passports. All "South Americans" were to be sent to a special internment camp, it was said, to be held there for a possible exchange against Germans in Latin America.

For a moment I saw hope again in my mother's eyes.

"Well, it would be nice . . . ," she said slowly. But her old fervor was gone.

My father shrugged his shoulders.

"Just another rumor," he said.

I tried to think what exchange to South America might mean. An end to prison life? Freedom? It was too much to comprehend. My thoughts had been hedged in barbed wire for so long that I could hardly imagine a normal life, particularly not in a place as far away and strange as South America.

For once a rumor proved to be true. Five days later the South American transport was officially announced. A special passenger train arrived to take us to a place called Bergen-Belsen. An exchange camp, the Germans said. The train consisted of a string of old, dilapidated third-class

137

carriages. But oh, what luxury compared to all those cattle cars!

When I saw them, I thought of Grannie, traveling in one of those boxcars on straw . . . and Ruthie . . . and all those others. Why us? I wondered . . . and I felt pleased and guilty at the same time. When we boarded the train, we were so conscious of Grannie's absence that this awareness almost blotted out all thoughts about leaving Westerbork.

I double-checked my rucksack to see if I had brought my notebooks along. Perhaps there would be times when I'd need them again, wherever we were going.

Bergen-Belsen

January 1944-January 1945

Chapter 12

THE TRAIN HAD HALTED for a long time. Inside the packed compartments we were waiting in darkness. Why the delay? Why had we stopped? Outside I could see nothing but snow —miles of moonlit snow stretching into the distance. Here and there the stark outlines of a tree or a clump of snow-covered bushes only accentuated the vast emptiness of the landscape.

"The Lunenburg Heath," someone whispered to me. "We can't be far. The camp is supposed to be near Celle, right in the middle of the heath."

We waited some more. I snuggled against my mother for warmth in the unheated train. The others were huddling too. While the train had been moving I hadn't felt the cold so much, but now, standing here in the darkness for hours, we felt the icy North German winter.

Suddenly there was a burst of steam from the engines. Slowly, the long train began to move forward. Then, shortly, it halted again. We had arrived. Outside our windows were the snow-covered platforms of a railroad station. Apparently we had been waiting just beyond it most of the night.

The station seemed ghostly and empty. Then suddenly it sprang to life. In spite of the war-time blackout, the large station lights came on, spilling huge round puddles of yellow light on the packed snow.

I heard loud voices, then I saw Germans, Gestapo officers in boots and leather coats, some of them holding bloodhounds on short chains.

"*Heraus, heraus* . . . get out. *Mach schnell* . . . hurry up . . . out of the train, everybody!"

The voices were rough, the tone menacing. Was this the special internment camp we had been promised? We looked at each other, not daring to ask.

I tumbled out of the train, stiff from the long, cramped ride. Behind me, an old man almost fell down the steep steps. My father grabbed him and then helped a young woman down who was staggering under the weight of her sleeping child. Someone began to throw luggage from the train windows, trying to unload the train as fast as possible. Rucksacks, bedrolls, suit-cases, landed on the platform, all mixed up. I scrambled for my belongings. Everyone did. These were the last few possessions we still owned.

"Leave those things, you'll get them at the

camp," a soldier ordered. "Old people and women with small children can ride on the trucks with the luggage. The rest of you will walk."

I noticed the trucks lined up on the road outside the station. Workmen wearing prison garb loaded the luggage onto the trucks.

We began to sort ourselves out. Those who could ride straggled toward the trucks with their crying children on their arms. My father, mother, and I lined up on the road with the others for the trek to the camp.

"I hope it's not too far," I whispered to my father. I felt terribly stiff. My parents and I had chosen to carry our rucksacks on our backs. We didn't want to be parted from our most essential belongings.

"If they are letting the old people ride it probably will be a long walk," my father said. "But it will feel good to stretch our legs after sitting in that compartment for hours. Stamp your feet, Rosie, to get the circulation going."

"Let's go, let's go," a soldier ordered impatiently. We started out — a long, straggling column of people trudging up a tree-shaded road through deep snow.

I walked along, inhaling the crisp, cold air. It felt good to my lungs after the stale, spent air of the train. It reminded me of the skiing vacations I had taken in snow-covered Austrian winter resorts. But I needed only to glance sideways to remember where I was. The German officers in their leather coats were walking alongside the column, their large, black dogs straining on their chains. The dogs looked so thin that I wondered when they had been fed last. They loped along, dark menacing shadows.

The column moved silently for we were all afraid to speak. I listened to the crunching sound our feet made on the crisp snow, the panting of the dogs, and the Germans' rough commands when someone lagged behind.

Above me the branches of the tall trees formed a tunnel across the road, blotting out most of the sky. But occasionally I could glimpse a lead-colored patch of sky and I knew that dawn was coming.

The straps of my rucksack bit into my shoulders. With each step the weight increased. I tugged at the straps with my hands, trying to ease the load for a few moments but instead I lost my balance. I swerved out of line. One of the dogs lunged at me. His hot breath was in my face, his menacing growl in my ear. I screamed. My father grabbed my arm and pulled me back.

"Stay in line," the guard shouted. "Keep on moving, we don't have all day!" He pulled the dog back on the heavy chain and patted the huge beast's head. "Good dog, Siegfried. Keep alert!"

I walked on, my knees like jelly, my eyes staring straight ahead. I didn't want to see that dog again. I felt my father's steadying hand on my elbow.

"Just hold on a little longer," he whispered. "It can't be very much farther now." And yet it seemed endless . . . step after step . . . as dawn slowly turned into day.

The sun was high in the sky when we finally reached the end of the long road. Before me the snow-covered roofs of the camp glistened in the sunlight. The guard, in his helmet and long gray uniform coat, opened the heavy gate. To either side, the strands of the barbed-wire fence stretched into the distance.

I walked on along a wide unpaved road which seemed to bisect the camp. On either side, barbed-wire enclosures marked different sections of the huge complex. Cages within a big cage, it seemed to me. People moved in these different compartments, some lining the fences and staring out at me. There were men in striped prison garb in one section, men and women in the remnants of tattered uniforms in another.

"They must be prisoners of war. Those are Russian uniforms," my mother whispered behind me.

I didn't answer. I couldn't believe what I saw. Again I wondered: Was this the special camp we had been told about. The place from which we might go to South America?

The camp road stretched on and on. Everywhere I saw rows of shedlike barracks built of unpainted wood. Neither trees nor shrubs relieved the barren spaces between the buildings. A strange silence hung over the place.

Finally we were led through another gate into a narrow enclosure. It was only two barracks wide, one for the men, one for the women. Before them, our suitcases and bedrolls and bundles were piled in the snow. I spotted my bedroll and ran to retrieve it.

We found the women and children who had come by truck inside the women's barracks. The old lady who had traveled in our compartment hugged me as if we had been parted for years. Some people had already found their belongings and spread blankets over the same old dirty straw mattresses.

My mother and I found two adjoining lower bunks and we flopped down on them, too exhausted for a moment to look for the rest of our bedding or to unpack. The mattress was lumpy and badly stained but I was too tired to care. In the bunk next to us a young mother was trying to soothe her crying twins. She was close to tears herself.

"They are hungry," she told me. "Hungry and cold. Our blankets and the bag with our food are outside, but I can't leave them long enough to look."

"I'll watch them for you," I offered. Gratefully, she slipped outside. The two toddlers didn't even seem to notice her absence. They just rocked back and forth on the lumpy mattress, their eyes swollen with tears, their thumbs in their mouths. And then, as if they had both reached utter exhaustion simultaneously, their whimpering died away and they fell asleep.

I was hungry. We all were. When two men in prison clothes brought food in a large galvanized iron vat a little later, I scrambled to find my enameled dinner bowl. It was hot soup — limp orange cubes of turnip swimming around in a pale, watery liquid. With it came small portions of black bread and ersatz coffee, a vile-tasting dark brown brew.

"Can you believe it — I miss the Westerbork food!" someone mumbled. I nodded. I had complained about the food in Westerbork, but now I longed for the substantial *stampot*, a thick mixture of potatoes mashed with vegetables.

Still, the food was hot and filled my empty stomach for the moment. I hunched on the edge of my bed, my hands cupped around my warm dinner bowl. Slowly my numbed fingers came back to life.

After lunch we organized. The two men who had been designated transport leaders back in Westerbork conferred with the Germans. They returned to report to us. These barracks, they told us, were only temporary quarters. A quarantine, of sorts. In a day or so, we would be moved to the much larger section next door. There we would be assigned permanent barracks and jobs.

My mother and I went outside. We wanted to see more of the new camp. Through the fence I could see the wooden barracks of the next camp in the distance. Between us lay an enormously large, flat, open space. It was covered with snow now but in the center of the huge field the snow was flattened and packed down hard.

I saw the people of the neighboring section for the first time early the next morning. From their barracks they walked out to the middle of the huge field and lined up in even rows.

They formed a square, facing inward, and in the middle two Gestapo officers paced back and forth. They seemed to be inspecting the rows but I didn't know what it was all about. They carried clubs and even across the distance I could hear their harsh voices barking commands.

Then the inspection was over, the people formed groups and marched toward the gate held open by a Gestapo guard. Up the camp road they went, beyond the point we had reached yesterday, until they disappeared from view.

"The work crews, probably," my father said. He had come from the men's barracks to join my mother and me at the fence. We had finished eating our breakfast, a ladleful of thin, pale gray gruel.

A little later I watched another group lining up on the big mustering square. These were the women and children and old people who did not have to work. The Gestapo officers kept them standing for a long time in their neat, even rows. Even the small children stood patiently in their places, sheltered a little from the icy wind by the taller adults behind them.

I peered at those strangers as if looking at them from a distance might tell me something about my new life. An old woman suddenly reminded me of Grannie, and I felt a stab of pain. Grannie was miles away, somewhere in Czechoslovakia. I wondered how she was doing. Had her camp been a disappointment too? I hoped things were better for her than they seemed to be here in Belsen.

This didn't look like the kind of place that might lead to freedom. Why had I ever let myself believe that something good might actually happen? This was just another German lie . . . another trap.

I went inside the barracks and stretched out on my bed. In a day or so I too would have to submit to the kind of routine I'd just witnessed. I wasn't looking forward to it.

In the barracks, people were moving around. Some were rummaging through their belongings, others were dressing or eating or fixing their beds. Cora, the young mother of the twins next to me, was sorting through a huge pile of dirty clothes and diapers.

"I'd better find a way to wash my laundry," she sighed. "The babies are sleeping. Now is my chance."

"I'll help you," I offered. I wanted to do something — anything.

"Oh, would you?" She smiled at me. I grabbed half of the laundry bundle and we set out for the washroom at the other end of the barracks.

Cora dumped her armful of diapers into one of the long galvanized sinks. She turned the handle and let the cold water trickle onto the clothes. There were several rows of these long sinks in the washroom, each with six or eight water taps. Other women were rinsing clothes in the cold water or washing themselves, stripped to the waist. They washed quickly and perfunctorily because it was freezing in the unheated room. The two toilets provided for nighttime use were already stopped up and overflowing. The room stank. I bent low over the washtub, concentrating on the stains in a pair of baby pants. Without soap even the hardest rubbing didn't help. Already my hands were red and wrinkled from plunging into the icy water.

I glanced at Cora, who was wringing out diapers with quick, practiced motions. Cora had lived in one of the large barracks in Westerbork and she was used to this kind of community washroom, to the discomfort of doing everything in a crowd. To me this was all new. It was as new as if I hadn't spent more than two years in Westerbork but had come to Belsen straight from Amsterdam. The acrid fumes of the outside latrine at the end of the compound made me gag. I froze when I saw those twenty women in a double row using the place at the same time.

My mother came looking for me, bundled up in her coat and scarf.

"The transport leader asked me and another woman to accompany them on an inspection of our new quarters over there in the other camp," she said. "The Germans want us to move tomorrow. They want us to get it all organized."

"I hope it's better than here," I mumbled.

"Don't count on it," my mother said. "I guess I'll be back in an hour or so. If you see your father, tell him where I went."

I went to the window and watched my mother and the others walking across the huge mustering square. I wondered what she'd find.

Beside me, Cora was folding the laundry. "I

wish we could hang it to dry outside," she said wistfully. There were no outside lines to hang it on, so we carried the wet things back into the barracks and hung them on the backs of our beds. A small iron stove in the middle of the barracks had been lighted now and gave off a little heat. The smoke mingled with all the other smells in the barracks, rising to the ceiling and hanging there like a murky cloud.

The sun had disappeared and it was snowing again. Large lacy snowflakes swirled outside the windows and covered the trampled, dirty snow on the ground with a fresh, clean layer. It clung to the little barbs of wire on the fences and to the tops of the wooden posts. Through the dancing flakes even the rough barracks in the distance looked different and mysterious and not quite so forbidding. I wished it would snow on and on for days and days.

The twins woke up from their nap and I started to play with them, romping on the beds. I didn't even hear my mother coming back until she called my name. There was an odd, strangled sound to her voice. I spun around. My mother stood there, not saying anything. Her face was contorted. Tears streamed down her cheeks. She let them run.

For a moment I couldn't move. I didn't know what to do. Then I ran to her side, putting my arms around her.

"What happened?" I asked hoarsely.

My mother let me lead her to the bed. She sat down heavily. From the other beds people looked at us curiously, but they left us alone. I grabbed my mother by the shoulders and shook her.

"What happened?" I pleaded.

"Grannie — it's Grannie," she said in a flat, dead voice.

"What about Grannie?" I cried.

"She's dead . . . she's dead!"

My mother cumpled against me and I held her close, trying to comfort her great, racking sobs.

Chapter 13

I COULDN'T BELIEVE Grannie had died. Grannie, so strong willed, so calmly accepting things, seemed invincible — eternal. Even when we moved to the main camp the following day and I heard the story myself from the people who had seen her die, I couldn't accept it.

The facts were simple. For no apparent reason, Grannie's transport had been routed to Belsen, held there for several weeks, and then, just as mysteriously, sent off again, presumably to its original destination. But Grannie had not gone with them. A couple of days before their departure she had suddenly died of a heart attack. There was no illness, no warning, no suffering. A sudden pain and she was gone.

The people who told us were Greek Jews from Salonica. We could tell that they had liked Grannie — they were sad about her death and sorry to bring us such bad news. Shyly they brought us some of the small keepsakes they had taken from her possessions — snapshots of my parents and me in round, silver frames, a small enameled pillbox, a scarf, some gloves, a cameo pin. They were a little embarrassed that they had these things. But there was no one to take charge of her possessions, they explained. After all, she had been alone.

We stared at the small heap of odds and ends they had brought us — all that we had left of Grannie now. A few possessions . . . and memory.

"Perhaps it was for the best," my father said. "How do we know what else she might have had to face. Who knows where that transport went next? Now at least we know that her death was quick."

I tried to remember what Grannie had told me about death. A new adventure, she had called it. Silently I prayed that it would be a happy adventure.

In a strange way Grannie seemed to reach out from death to ease our first few days in the new camp. Because of her, we became friendly with some of the Greek women. In Belsen the Greeks enjoyed the same kind of privilege the "old camp" had enjoyed in Westerbork. They were in charge of the camp administration, the labor supply, the food distribution. We were fortunate to find friends among the Greeks.

They too, like the "old camp," were a clannish group, suspicious of outsiders. Yet Grannie had made friends with them. Perhaps it was because she spoke fluent French and the Greeks used French to communicate with outsiders. Luckily my mother knew the language too. That helped to break the ice.

The Greek women found good beds for us near their own in the huge barracks and they gave advice. They told us which Gestapo officers were dangerous and which were easier going; what work squads were best and which were worst; and how to get into the better ones during the early-morning labor shape-up on the big mustering square.

Labor service was compulsory for all camp inmates from fifteen to sixty-five. Only the very old, the severely handicapped, and mothers of very young children were exempt.

When I started to get ready for the labor shape-up the first morning, my mother held me back.

"You stay here, Rosie," she said. "You don't have to go."

"But I'm over fifteen," I argued.

"You don't look older than thirteen or fourteen. The Greeks told me that the labor bosses as well as the Germans go by looks. Nobody will check how old you really are. The Greek women advised me not to let you go to the shape-up."

"That's cheating," I said, aghast.

"For heavens' sake, grow up, Rosie! You should be grateful that you look young enough to escape labor service. Do you really think it's wrong to fool the people who imprison us? You are fourteen, when anybody asks you. Remember that."

I stayed, but I felt guilty and rebellious. I didn't like to look younger than my fifteen years. Now here I was, almost grown-up, and yet I was to be counted among the children.

Still, it was rather pleasant to get back under the covers for another hour instead of braving the chill and darkness of the mustering square at six A.M. It was daylight and a good deal warmer when the rest of us straggled out to the big square for our turn at being counted. We lined up in rows of five and waited for the interminable counting. First the barracks leader counted us, and then one of the Greek supervisors. Finally the SS official made his own rounds. He was a florid-faced, heavyset man with red hair and a deep scowl. Stomping along, he glared at us, impatiently tapping his high, shiny boots with the riding crop he carried in his hand.

"That's Red Müller," someone whispered behind me. "He's the worst of the lot."

As he approached our group, I felt myself cringing. My head was down. Surely Red Müller would know my true age if he saw my face. I waited fearfully to be pulled out of my place, to be denounced as an impostor. But nothing happened. Even to the malevolent eyes of Red Müller I didn't look fifteen years old.

"Don't think you missed anything," my mother told me, when she came back from her first day's work looking tired and wan. "Piles of muddy army boots to be cut into usable pieces of sole or upper leather. Look at my hands — full of blisters. You'd never have the strength to cut through that heavy leather with the dull knives they give us. Just be glad you can stay here in the camp."

How could I explain to her that I felt glad and guilty at the same time? I didn't try. Instead I told her about my day. I had helped to sweep the barracks and scrub the wooden tables in the small "day room" at one end of the barracks. With some of the other older girls I had minded a group of younger children who grew restless during the long, boring day. In Belsen the sleeping section of the barracks had to be kept perfectly neat during the day. There was always the threat of a sudden inspection.

My father had fared the worst of all of us. He was utterly exhausted when he came to see us after supper that first evening. He had been put into the dreaded logging detail, which involved hard physical labor. Daddy had never cut down a tree or chopped wood in his whole life. He wondered how he could possibly keep up the pace.

As the days passed we worried more and more about my father. The SS guards had no patience with unskilled workers. They were quick with their whips and clubs and my father received more than his share of the blows. After just one week he looked gaunt and ill. We were terribly worried that he wouldn't be able to last much longer.

My mother spoke to her Greek friends and they said they would try to help. A few days later the Greek labor boss took my father out of the logging detail. He was put on the food distribution squad. Its task was to bring the huge vats of soup or ersatz coffee from the distant camp kitchens each day. This was hard work too, but at least my father wasn't beaten in his new labor gang. Slowly he regained his strength.

For me, time passed slowly in Belsen. The routine was deadly. Sweeping the barracks, keeping the children quiet, standing for hours on *Appell*—the daily roll call. On rainy days the counting always seemed to take longer, the figures wouldn't agree, the number was short. Red Müller would shout at the Greek camp leader, who in turn shouted at the barracks leaders. Someone scurried away to count the sick in the barracks again.

"I bet they didn't count one of the dead again," old Mrs. Herera muttered behind me. She was one of the few Greeks who didn't have an excuse for the *Appell*. Another was little Albertico, the seven-year-old Greek orphan who was haphazardly cared for by all the Greek women in turn. Albertico had no one to rub his frostbitten fingers or to kiss away his tears when his toes hurt after standing still in the snow for an hour or so. But he was a brave little fellow and he seldom complained.

Next to me, thirteen-year-old Steffi was playing word games with her ten-year-old sister Lisa. For Lisa, standing still so long was pure agony. In addition, her only shoes were nearly a size too small by now and there was just no way of getting new ones in Belsen. How grateful I was for my own sturdy ski boots. They still just fit. I prayed that my feet had reached their full size so that I would not outgrow them.

The shrill whistles of the foremen signaled the end of the roll call. Lisa was crying by now with pain and I helped Steffi partly carry her little sister back to the barracks. How gentle Steffi was with the younger child. She never seemed to think of her own fatigue. The girls' parents were far away in Australia, separated from their children by mischance and by war. It was up to Steffi to care for Lisa until they could be reunited again after the war.

Inside the barracks, a small knot of children had gathered around the bed of the Greek camp leader's wife. The attraction was Sigurd, their baby son, who daily at this time had his precious bottle of formula. Only Sigurd, among all the children, was lucky enough to get milk every day. Now he lay contentedly on the pink silk bedspread, a visible but incongruous symbol of camp privilege.

Paula, another Greek orphan who was used by the family of the camp leader as their special drudge, supervised the bottle ritual. Afterwards it was her privilege to give the dregs of the bottle to one of the greedily watching children. Even the smallest sip was a coveted treat. It tasted rich and sweet and it was a far cry from turnip soup. I knew, because I'd had my share another morning when I had drained the baby's bottle to the last delectable drop.

Watching Sigurd with his milk made the rest

of us hungry. When we heard the clanking of the soup vats in the day room a little later, everybody rushed into line. I held back a little. I was beginning to learn the trick of waiting to join the line until one of the vats was nearly empty. Even though the barracks leader stirred the soup constantly with her long ladle, the heavier pieces had a way of sinking to the bottom. My reward for gauging it just right was a few cubes of potato among the turnips. It made my day.

But such little triumphs really couldn't brighten the grayness of everyday life. Everything was gray in Belsen: the buildings, the road, the plowed strip of earth beyond the electric fences. After a while I envied the workers who could march out of the wide gates of the camp every day. The work barracks were not far, but at least they were a change of scenery.

Finally I too got a chance. Along with a group of girls as young as twelve I was sent from the roll call on a trip to the work barracks. Some extra hands were needed that day. I hardly could wait to see what lay outside our compound but as we walked up the road I found that this part of the camp looked exactly like the part we could see from behind our own fences. Just more unpainted wooden sheds and more barbed wire.

I found "Shoes" just as my mother had described it. A huge, badly ventilated shed where we sat on benches around large tables piled high with muddy, outworn boots. And mother was right, my hands lacked the strength to cut through the tough pieces of leather. The forelady came around a few times to show me, but it was no use. Finally, with a sigh, she beckoned me from the table. The work leader had agreed to send me next door to another shed called "Uniforms." The work and the surroundings were similar. Only here the long tables held heaps of torn, worn German army uniforms. The task was to rip the seams and salvage the usable pieces of fabric.

I congratulated myself for having escaped "Shoes" for that day until I reached for the next piece and found myself handling a badly torn uniform shirt caked with black splotches of dried blood. I nearly dropped the shirt when I realized the significance of the gaping hole and the black stains around it. My stomach heaved and I was afraid that I would throw up right there over all the pieces of gray uniform.

"Another German bit the dust," the woman next to me whispered with obvious satisfaction. But I couldn't rid myself of the image of some young soldier dying of his horrendous wound somewhere on a distant battlefield. After that I handled the pieces of uniform gingerly, all too aware of where they had come from.

That first glimpse into the world of the work details showed me that my lot wasn't that bad after all. I no longer envied the people who had to sit day after day in those dusty sheds, working for hours with bleeding and blistered fingers. But I still felt out of place and uneasy among the mothers and children in the barracks. I didn't even have a younger child like Steffi or Paula to be responsible for.

In the spring several more transports arrived. The newcomers brought grim news. Westerbork was rapidly being emptied, its usefulness as a transit center having come to an end. This meant that hardly any Jews remained in Holland who had not been taken to one camp or another.

As for the war, they knew as little as we. In fact, we could tell them about the daily squadrons of American and British planes that crossed the German skies in broad daylight with apparent impunity. It was a thrill to see those little white dots gliding slowly through the blue sky above us. But it was best not to let one of the German guards see us scanning the skies. Still, even if we didn't look, the noise of the planes was there. An unmistakable droning, like a secret message to us that there still was another world outside of Germany.

The new transports brought quite a few members of the Youth Group. But I avoided them all. The girls I had known had been put into work squads right away. I didn't want to explain to them why I wasn't working.

One day my mother got sick. The first day she dragged herself to work even though she was hot with fever. She had recently been put into a new work squad, the clean-up squad, which went to clean the SS quarters every morning. It was hard, nerve-racking work because they had to work under constant German surveillance. But now and then the women did find some edible food in the garbage pails which they shared during an occasional unguarded moment, and on such days my mother could give me or my father an extra bit of her bread ration. It worried her that she felt sick. She didn't want to lose her place on this special detail.

But the next day her fever was worse.

"You'd better go to the clinic for a doctor's excuse," our barracks leader counseled. "He might give you something for the fever. Even that army doctor will see that you are really sick."

"But my job?" my mother argued. "I don't want to give it up."

"Could I go for you?" I asked.

My mother looked surprised. Then she shook her head.

"No, Rosie. It's too rough. You couldn't take it. Working under the eyes of the Gestapo guards is frightening . . . dangerous."

"Your forelady will have to take someone else into the squad," our barracks leader said.

I grabbed my coat. Suddenly I was determined to go. I wasn't a child. I had to save my mother's place on the squad.

"Don't go, Rosie," my mother cried.

But I had to.

Chapter 14

IT WASN'T WINTER anymore, but it was still quite dark outside at six A.M. Shadowy figures moved past me through the darkness, hurrying toward the mustering square. I joined the crowd. It was hard to find where I belonged. People were milling about, finding their squads or joining the group of temporarily unassigned workers. At the guardhouse near the gate two German officers stood silhouetted against the light streaming out the open door. One of them held a dog on a chain, the first bloodhound I had seen since the day we arrived.

I was confused and began to worry that I might not find my mother's squad until I spotted Mrs. Rossau, my mother's squad leader. She seemed doubtful about my taking my mother's place, and for a moment I thought she would send me back. She could always get someone from the unassigned workers.

"Please, let me try today," I pleaded. I think Mrs. Rossau started to say no, but just then the whistles began to blow to signal line-up time. Mrs. Rossau shrugged her shoulders.

"Oh, all right," she said. "Come along. But stay with me and do just what I tell you."

We marched out the gate and turned right, toward the entrance of the camp. The officers' barracks was outside the main gate. I tried to recognize things I had seen on the day of our arrival, but in the darkness the buildings were just shadowy outlines.

"Stay close, Rosemarie," Mrs. Rossau whispered when we entered the German mess hall. I looked around curiously.

It was a huge room, bare and austere. Rows and rows of wooden tables surrounded by wooden chairs. Bare walls, plain wooden plank floors. At one end of the room a wide counter divided the dining hall from the kitchen. Beyond it, prisoners in their striped shirts were just beginning to wash piles of breakfast dishes. Trays still heaped with slices of white bread made my mouth water. I hadn't seen white bread for years.

"Don't even look at that bread," Mrs. Rossau whispered tersely. "And watch out for guards. They'd just love to catch one of us stealing something. Just remember that, Rosemarie, we don't take anything."

As if to prove her words, a rather young German soldier walked into the mess hall at that moment. He carried a tommy gun. Glancing insolently at our small group still huddled together near the entrance, he took up his station in front of the bread.

"Well, what are you waiting for?" he shouted. "On with it — on with it — get going with the work."

Mrs. Rossau handed me a rough broom, just bundles of twigs tied to a long handle. "Start sweeping," she said. "Do the best you can — they don't give us good cleaning equipment."

I started to sweep down the aisle, painfully aware that the guard kept watching me. Perhaps he realized that I wasn't one of the regular workers.

The other women had scattered. Some had gone to clean the officers' sleeping quarters in the next building, others were scrubbing the tables or cleaning the washrooms at the end of the hall. Mrs. Rossau was the only one still near me, sweeping the other side of the room.

The guard was pacing up and down, cradling his gun in his bent arm. Each time I looked up he seemed nearer to me. Finally, just as I was sweeping past the big iron stove in the middle of the mess hall, he was standing beside me, barring my way. I didn't look up at him, but I could almost feel his eyes boring into me.

"Come over here, girl," he commanded. "I've been watching you — just pushing the dust around with that broom. That stove is full of ashes. Get down and clean it out. That will give you something to sweep away."

In a panic, I went down on my knees in front of the black iron stove, my hands trembling. I opened the little door. Inside, the grate was indeed heaped with a load of dead gray ashes. I looked around for something to clean it out with. The guard guessed what I was looking for.

"Use your hands, use your hands," he snarled. "What's the matter, afraid to get your hands dirty? That's where you belong, you little Jewish brat, wallowing in the dirt."

Blinking back tears, I began to sweep handfuls of ashes out of the grate. The ashes were still warm, but not hot enough to burn me. But he couldn't have known that, I thought in fury. He wanted me to get burned!

He was still standing over me, so close that I could feel his legs touching my back. Once I looked up and I saw his eyes, steely gray eyes, staring at me in such an odd way, as if he were measuring me with them. I went back to my ashes, trying to control my trembling. He mustn't know how scared I am, I thought. I don't want him to have that pleasure.

Suddenly Mrs. Rossau was standing next to us. She carried a dustpan and a hand broom.

"Can I do anything here?" she asked pleasantly. "Is there a problem with the stove? Perhaps I can help."

The guard stepped back so quickly that he almost stumbled over my feet.

"Just get on with this, get on with it," he ordered gruffly. "Get that mess cleaned up." He strode away, then took up his position again, leaning on his gun.

"Let me do this, Rosemarie," Mrs. Rossau said. "Just go on sweeping toward the washrooms. You can clean up in there if you do it quickly enough not to get caught. We're not supposed to use these washrooms, only clean them. But you'll have a chance to rinse your hands."

I went on sweeping. The guard was still looking at me. Keeping my head averted, I pushed past him, clutching my broom hard to control the trembling in my hands. That horrible guard! Why did he have to pick on me? Was this the kind of trouble my mother had meant with her warnings? Well, I'd cope with it. I'd show her I could manage. I'd show them all.

Before me, on the wooden floor, something glistened. Automatically I leaned over and picked it up. It was a needle, an ordinary sewing needle. I turned it around in my hands, looking at it.

Mrs. Rossau again materialized at my side.

"What did you find?" she asked anxiously. "Put it down on the nearest table. It's best not to be seen picking anything up."

We looked around, toward the guard, but he suddenly seemed to have lost interest in me. He had walked over to the window, turning his back to us.

"Does he always stare at people like this?" I whispered.

"Only at young, pretty girls," Mrs. Rossau whispered back with a smile. "That's why we prefer to have just older women on this squad. It's safer that way."

We reached the washrooms and Mrs. Rossau pushed me inside. Two of our women were in there, scrubbing the floor on their knees. One of them waved a scrap of torn newspaper at us.

"Some bits of news, only one week old," she said. "The Allies seem to be doing well in North Africa."

Mrs. Rossau pointed to the stacks of cut-up newspaper inside the toilet cubicles. "Our news bureau," she said. "Even the Germans are short of toilet paper now."

The other woman beckoned to me. "Take my place scrubbing," she said. "Then you can have your share of the spoils." She pulled a slice of bread out of her blouse and gave it to me. "We found this in a garbage pail. If a guard comes in, you hide it under your floor rags. This is the safest place to have this snack — inside the cubicle, with your back to the room."

The bread was white and dry with a dusting of green mold around the edges. But I didn't care — it was bread. I wolfed my piece down in big, greedy bites, hardly aware of what I was eating, listening with each bite for the guard to catch me with my mouth full.

I wished that I could close the door of the cubicle behind me for one brief moment of total privacy. Would I ever again know the luxury of being alone?

I closed my eyes and I saw the camp days stretching before me — day after day of hunger and dirt and boredom and pain. Had I ever known things like a real bed, a warm bath, an easy chair — or a clean, neat, tiled washroom like this? Had I? In this life — or in another?

It scared me to realize how I had sunk into passive acceptance of an intolerable situation, bearing everything meted out to me, living only for the next breath, the next heartbeat, for another moment of life.

It was better not to remember. It made daily life bearable.

By the time we were ready to march back to the camp later that day I was utterly exhausted. My back hurt from handling the awkward broom, my knees were sore from all that unaccustomed kneeling. But I felt good. I had done a day's work — a woman's day's work.

We were just about to enter the gate of our camp when a German staff car roared up behind us. Red Müller jumped out of the car, waving his arms.

"Stop the thieves," he shouted. "These women are thieves. They must be searched. They have stolen from the mess hall."

Mrs. Rossau stepped forward. "Please, may I ask what is missing?" she said politely. "Perhaps my women have seen it. Perhaps they know where it is."

"Needles," Red Müller shouted again. "Precious sewing needles. The guard saw one of you pick them up. You'd better return them — and now. On the double!"

The women looked at each other. They didn't know what Red Müller was talking about. But I did. I remembered putting the needle on one of the tables and Mrs. Rossau's anxious glance at the guard. So he had seen me after all. Even though he had turned his back to me right afterwards.

Mrs. Rossau remembered too.

"One needle was found," she announced. "It

was left on one of the tables. One of my workers picked it up from the floor."

"There were two needles," Red Müller roared. "Don't think you can get away with a pack of lies. Two needles were left in the dining hall. And you'd better produce them."

"Perhaps if I went to look," Mrs. Rossau suggested. Red Müller waved his assent. Mrs. Rossau started to walk back to the mess hall with a gun-toting guard at her heels. The rest of us stood and waited. Red Müller remained with us. He was stomping up and down, his hands behind his back. We stood silently, in neat rows of five, our arms at our side.

It seemed forever until Mrs. Rossau returned. But when she did, we could see from the grim expression on her face that her mission had not been successful. Even the one needle I had put on the table had vanished by now. Perhaps it had rolled to the floor again and disappeared into one of the wide cracks between the floorboards. Or perhaps the guard had taken it and then accused us of theft. We couldn't guess.

"If you can't return those needles – no bread for the entire camp for three days," Red Müller roared. His face had turned red with rage, a shade redder even than the carroty shade of his hair. I just stared. Three days without bread! And it was all my fault. If I had only left that needle on the floor or swept it away with the dust! I felt that I should do something. But what?

Then Mrs. Rossau approached the angry German.

"Perhaps we could replace the needles," she offered. "I might have one among my things in the camp. Perhaps someone else has a needle too. If you will permit me to look, I'll replace those needles."

"Ten needles," Red Müller said. "Ten needles — and quick. I'll teach you thieves a lesson. Ten needles, or the whole camp will be without bread. Ten needles, and I think that's a generous offer!"

The guard opened the gate and let Mrs. Rossau hurry inside. The rest of us remained in formation outside on the road. I hardly dared to breathe. I twisted my skirt. The time seemed endless. Where would Mrs. Rossau find the needles? Few people in the camp still possessed such luxuries.

It was nearly dark when the gate opened and Mrs. Rossau appeared holding out ten needles stuck into a piece of paper. Red Müller counted them with agonizing slowness.

"March on inside," he ordered curtly, looking at each of us in turn. "And let that be a lesson to you — thieves will not be tolerated in this camp."

By the time I returned to my barracks, my mother had heard about the incident at the gate. She was at the barracks door, waiting for me. When she saw me, she reached out for me with a sigh of relief.

"Thank God, you are back safely," she said. "I should have stopped you from going. That squad isn't for you. You need strong nerves to deal with the Germans face to face."

"It was all my fault," I said. "Perhaps if I hadn't picked up that needle, the guard wouldn't have noticed — they wouldn't have thought about needles. I just gave them a chance."

"No, it wasn't your fault," my mother said. "If they want to find something to harass us, they can always find something with which to find fault."

"I'll do better tomorrow," I said.

"You won't go again, tomorrow," my mother said. "I took some medicine and my fever is gone. Anyway, the doctor gave me only a one-day exemption from work. So I will go myself again tomorrow."

I looked at my mother and I saw the fine lines of fatigue around her eyes and the streaks of gray that had crept into her blond hair. She didn't look fit to go out with the squad tomorrow. But there was no arguing with the verdict of the camp doctor. If he declared a person fit to work, that was the final word.

I turned away. I didn't want my mother to read the relief in my eyes. I should have felt sorry that I couldn't spare my mother one extra day of going to work. But I couldn't help feeling thoroughly relieved that I wouldn't have to face that arrogant young guard in the mess hall again tomorrow. Tomorrow I would be sheltered again in the comparative comfort and safety of the barracks.

Was my mother right after all? Was I immature? Did I belong with the children? I didn't like those thoughts.

Chapter 15

IT WAS YOM KIPPUR, the Day of Atonement. And it was a beautiful warm September day.

"Do you remember how Grannie used to say that the sun always shines on the Jewish high holy days?" Mother asked me as she was getting ready for work that morning. Of course everyone was expected to work as usual even on the most important Jewish holiday. Those who were most orthodox in their religious beliefs marked the day with prayer and fasting anyway. It meant going to work without even the usual thin slice of coarse bread.

Later, during counting roll call, an announcement was made: bath day today! Everyone line up with your towels at the gate right after the roll call.

I could almost feel the undercurrent of dismay all around me. Bath day on Yom Kippur! Leave it to the SS to find something to harass us with on this day of religious dedication. Normally everyone would have welcomed the chance to stand under a warm shower for a few minutes on this pleasant, summery day. It was a treat we had enjoyed only a few times in the nine months since we had come to Belsen. But to the more religious among us, enjoying this today would be a sacrilege.

When I reached the gate a little later I spotted Sarah, a girl I had known in Westerbork. We lined up together with our towels and hoarded bits of soap. I rather looked forward to our little outing, religious holiday or not. It was a change in routine, a longed-for luxury. I couldn't wait to wash the dirt and grime out of my hair under running warm water.

Next to me, Sarah looked pained. Sarah came from a deeply orthodox family and she was fasting today.

"I hope I won't faint in the shower," she complained. "I feel sort of dizzy already. I had hoped I could sit around quietly most of today."

"Do you really think a small piece of bread would have made a difference?" I asked. I'd had my breakfast in the morning, but I felt hungry again just the same. That wasn't unusual. I'd gotten used to being hungry all the time. It wasn't the sharp, nagging kind of hunger I used to feel when a meal was late and my stomach angrily tried to remind me of my neglect. This hunger was a constant companion, a deep-rooted feeling of emptiness. Perversely, it made me think of food all the time. The feeling was worst right after a meal because our rations of bread and turnip soup just weren't enough to satisfy us.

"Try not to think about food," I advised Sarah. "I'm sure that dizzy feeling is mostly in your mind anyway, because you *know* you're fasting today."

"How can I with those two behind us?" Sarah whispered back. I had to laugh. The two women in line behind us were engaged in one of the favorite camp pastimes: exchanging recipes. "Cooking," the women called it, and everybody I knew was doing it all the time.

Those two behind us now were deep in an argument about the best method of making chocolate soufflé.

"I always use eight eggs," the taller one insisted. "And at least two ounces of butter for each egg. You have to beat the butter well before you add the eggs — that's part of the secret."

Butter, chocolate, eggs! Were there really such things? Frankly, my own daydreams didn't run to such luxuries. I dreamed of more prosaic things, such as heaping plates of fried potatoes. The way Grannie used to fry them in lots of butter. Potatoes until I couldn't eat any more.

The guard opened the gate and our line moved forward. Once again I watched for the landmarks as we walked along: the Russian camp, the kitchen complex, the political prisoner compound. The bath house lay just inside the main gate — a large structure of red brick topped by a tall chimney.

Inside the men and women separated. The men went to the right, the women to the left. In the large women's dressing room I sat down on one of the benches to remove my clothes. I folded them into a wire basket, which I handed in at a counter on our way to the shower room. While we bathed, the basket with clothes would be fumigated to kill whatever vermin they might contain. It was really a futile gesture because everything we owned back in the camp still remained as vermin-ridden as ever. But I had accepted a long time ago that few things done in the camp ever made any sense.

We lined up naked before the shower room, clutching our towels and pieces of soap. The last time I had been here it had been winter and the wait in the poorly heated hall had been unpleasantly chilly. Today it wasn't too bad. Sarah and I waited together. We were with the third group admitted to the showers. The women shoved and pushed to find places under the twenty or so shower heads — four or five of us to each one. The water came in a tepid trickle and I soaped up hurriedly because our turn under the shower would be brief. Above us, on a catwalk, an SS guard walked back and forth with a rifle against his shoulder. I wondered why the Germans felt that a group of naked women and children had to be guarded so carefully with a gun. The guard was young. His face was totally expressionless. I looked at him curiously while I scrubbed my hair. Did it embarrass him to be in the room with so many undressed women? Or had he become used to the sight, just as I accepted his presence simply as part of the situation?

And yet, we must be an odd sight, I decided, as I looked around me — a bunch of scarecrows, bedraggled and thin. I looked at Sarah, who had been slightly too plump way back in Westerbork. Now her arms and legs were like matchsticks and her ribs stuck out like ridges on her chest. There were no mirrors in the camp and I hadn't seen my own body for a long time. Were my own arms and legs as thin and angular as hers? My hands moved to explore my ribs and the bony points of my elbows. Of course they were, and no wonder. The food in the camp was getting less and less all the time. It had been months since we had gotten a second meal of gruel in the day. And I could hardly remember the last small rations of margarine or jam. Now it was just turnip soup and bread. The bread was given out only once a week — a depressingly small portion — and it took a lot of will power to hoard it day by day under our mattresses instead of gobbling it all up right away.

Our time under the shower was up and we went out into another room to dry off and to wait for our clothes to come back from the fumigation chamber. They came back warm and smelling of disinfectant, and they made me feel clean and fresh for a change. A small pleasure to be savored.

On our way back we heard the droning of

the Allied planes overhead and the sound added to my moment of contentment. As long as the planes flew we knew that the war was still on — that there was still hope for an Allied victory. I sent a silent prayer up to those planes high in the sky. Please come and rescue us, I prayed, hurry up and bring us liberation. Did any of those American flyers up there guess what hope and joy he brought us? Could he spot our rows of barracks from his great height and did he realize what kind of a place he was flying over? Probably not. Most likely he was intent on his distant target and the rows of buildings in our camp were just an unimportant fleck of enemy territory. Perhaps nobody in the whole wide world knew or cared that we were here. Or if they knew, they had forgotten.

Back in the barracks we lined up for our soup. Sarah had crept into a little corner, trying to blot out the sight and smell of the food. Even the sound of the ladle against the soup bowls made her own fast almost unbearable. Seeing her suffer made me feel guilty for enjoying my own meal.

"Please, Sarah, do eat something," I pleaded. "Fasting just isn't practical here in the camp."

Sarah looked longingly toward the soup vats. "My father would kill me if he found out," she said. "Fasting on this one day is supposed to be a sacrifice."

"And what does it do for God if you kill yourself with your sacrifices?" I asked angrily. But Sarah didn't respond. We had been over this ground before — it was an old argument between us — but one I wasn't likely to win.

I shrugged my shoulders. "Just go ahead and be stubborn," I told her. I was angry that she was hurting herself.

Sarah and her family had had to give up things like kosher food a long time ago, but for the rest they kept as strictly to their orthodox beliefs as circumstances would allow. And that included fasting on Yom Kippur.

Shortly after Yom Kippur the weather turned colder. We began to prepare ourselves for another harsh North German winter. My father, who had been in and out of the hospital barracks all summer, got sick again and was taken to the infirmary for the fourth time. This time he had pneumonia, a serious matter since he was weakened by the bouts of yellow jaundice and typhoid fever he had just passed through. My mother and I watched him get thinner and more waxen in his face day by day. If there were only something we could do! Finally my mother traded in our last two precious cans of condensed milk for a few of the life-saving sulfa tablets the Greek doctor had smuggled into the camp from Salonica. He was hoarding them jealously for his own people but my mother persuaded him to trade some to her.

There was a lot of sickness in the camp. Camp fever, we called it, but knowledgeable people whispered that it was a typhus epidemic. There were many deaths. One day Steffi's little sister, Lisa, died. She was taken to the hospital barracks but it was too late. I watched Steffi walking behind the cart that carried the coffins of the dead to the crematorium. She was permitted to follow the cart only to the gate. The same coffins were used again and again. And each trip the cart made there were more of them piled on it and it was followed by more mourners.

One of Cora's twins died too, and Mrs. Herera, the old Greek lady I had liked best among all the Greeks. Camp fever struck indiscriminately.

It was terrible watching Steffi in her grief. She moved among us like a robot, her eyes dull, her voice listless. The day Lisa died we had just received our weekly bread rations and Steffi returned to the barracks with Lisa's things, including her untouched piece of bread. I watched her holding it in her hands, turning it around and around, staring at it. A whole week's bread ration — and now it was hers, her inheritance from her little sister.

Finally she couldn't bear it any longer. She took her knife and sliced the bread and began to eat it slice by slice until it was all gone. And throughout that whole awesome funeral meal tears were rolling down her cheeks. We all watched Steffi, but no one interfered. It was her own private ceremony of mourning.

I think there were moments when I didn't really believe in all those deaths, when I pretended that the people would return — that it was all a bad dream from which I would awaken when the war was over. It scared me to see everything breaking down like this, to watch people wearing out and giving up the struggle. I clung to my parents, grateful each morning that we were all three still alive. And it was reassuring to watch my mother's grim determination to keep it that way for another day. Survival had become my mother's religion, and my father and I were carried along by her zeal.

One day, early in November, we noticed a great deal of activity going on in the wide, open area between the end of our camp and the work barracks in the distance. Convict workmen were clearing the ground and putting up rows and rows of huge, gray tents. We wondered who and what would be housed under the ugly, coarse canvas.

We found out the next morning. A long column of women straggled into the camp, limping up the camp road past our compound and into the tent camp next door. They wore striped cotton prison dresses and their heads were shaved and many of them had no shoes. They hobbled along barefoot or with muddy and bloody rags around their feet.

At first there was no contact between the newcomers and us. The strip of no-man's-land between our barbed-wire fence and theirs was carefully patrolled by armed SS guards. The first news about the tent camp women trickled in from the workers returning from "Shoes" and "Uniforms." The area near their latrine was not so carefully patrolled and they were able to shout across to the tent camp women and get shouted replies in return.

The women had come all the way from Poland,

from the camp named Auschwitz, of which we knew very little but the name. They had been pulled out of Auschwitz ahead of the advancing Russian armies and been dragged all the way across Germany, mostly on foot. The women here were the survivors — the ones that hadn't died along the way.

We watched them through the barbed wire, moving to and fro among their tents, lining up for food or water. We had seen them arriving and we knew they had no possessions except for the thin prison dress they wore. At night they slept on the bare ground under the tent canvas, perhaps rolled into the single thin army blanket each had been issued when they arrived. They carried these blankets wherever they went, draping them around their shoulders like shawls against the cold November winds or sitting on them when they squatted on the ground, eating from the few dinner bowls they had to share among them.

It was painful to watch them but somehow I, like everyone else, was drawn to the fence again and again. Shivering in my ski pants and winter coat, I wondered how these women survived without proper shelter or clothing.

I'd once heard an old English saying: "Here but for the grace of God go I," and those words kept running through my head. In some giant game of chance I had been lucky and was here on this side of the fence instead of on the other. How rich we were compared to these women — rich in the clothes we still owned, in the dignity conferred upon us by such simple possessions as a toothbrush and a comb, or even hair to use it on! And we were rich in the families that still surrounded us, people whom we loved and who loved us and for whom we wanted to go on living.

The women in the tent camp had been reduced to the simplest form of existence. But above all, each was alone. And that surely was their greatest tragedy.

Every day more of the tent camp women kept arriving. They were of a half dozen different nationalities. The yellow stars they wore even on their prison dresses labeled them as Jews in a variety of languages: *Jood, Jude, Juif* . . . the list was long.

Eventually the Germans stopped patrolling between our two camps all the time and we began to make contact. Names were called across, people trying to find out if loved ones were on one side or the other. Sometimes people discovered friends or relatives on the tent side and then they would throw clothing or even food across the wire whenever the guard was out of the way.

I kept going back to the fence, scanning the faces on the other side for a familiar one. And then one day I spotted her! A heart-shaped face and big blue eyes — it was Ruthie. Ruthie Schoenheim from Westerbork. Even without her hair and in her shapeless prison dress I couldn't mistake her. Ruthie saw me too and her face lit up and she waved to me.

"Fancy meeting you here!" she called across

and there was something of the old bravado in her voice and in her smile. But her face looked haggard under her shaved skull and her eyes didn't smile at all.

We reached out toward each other through the wire fences but the distance was too far and we could just stand there and stare, each held back within her own particular cage.

My mother was with me and she broke the silence.

"Are you all right, Ruthie?" she asked, calling us back to practical matters.

Ruthie shrugged her shoulders. "Nobody here is all right," she said. "But I'm hanging on. I'm doing as well as can be expected."

"Wait here, Ruthie," I said. "I'll get some things for you." I turned and ran back to my barracks and started to rummage feverishly through my things, trying to find something Ruthie could use. She had no shoes, but neither had I except for the ski boots I wore, and besides Ruthie's feet were bigger. I pulled a green and white sweater out of my rucksack. Grannie had knitted it for me — it was something to remember her by. But Ruthie needed it more than I. I ran back to the fence. Ruthie was still waiting there, talking in snatches with my mother. It was hard to talk with so many people calling across the fence all at the same time. Also, they were pushing and shoving for a spot from which they could see better.

I threw the sweater, and the first time it got caught on our fence and I tore the sleeve of my coat as I reached up to retrieve it. The second time it went across and landed in no-man's-land. Oh, please, let no one else get it first, I thought, but Ruthie went down on her hands and knees and pulled it in under the lowest strand of wire. She slipped into the sweater and hugged herself tight, and this time the smile came from her eyes too.

We met again the next day but I couldn't throw over the scarf I had brought because the SS guard appeared suddenly, stopping all conversations. We could just stand there and look at each other in silence. Ruthie had come with a friend this time, a petite little thing with wisps of pale blond hair just beginning to grow back on her head. They stood there, huddled together against the wind, and then they finally waved and walked back together toward their tents. They walked very slowly and it seemed to me that Ruthie was leaning on her companion.

The next day Ruthie did not appear nor the next nor the one after that. Then on the fourth day I spotted the green and white sweater farther down the fence and ran over, waving. But it wasn't Ruthie. It was her small, blond friend, wearing my sweater.

"Where is Ruthie?" I shouted at her. She looked up and recognized me, but her face remained without any expression.

"Ruthie is dead," she said. "She died yesterday."

"But she can't be dead," I cried, gripping the wire. "She was walking when I saw her last. She can't be dead. You're lying!"

"No, no," the girl said. "She was sick for a long time. She just didn't want it to be true. But yesterday she only wanted to sleep. She slept and slept. I went to get food for both of us. But when I came back, she was stiff and cold. She died in her sleep."

I didn't answer. I couldn't say anything. I stared at the girl — that strange girl, Ruthie's friend — who was wearing the sweater Ruthie should be wearing.

The girl pulled the sweater tighter around herself, as if she guessed what I was thinking.

"I took it. Ruthie didn't need it anymore," she said simply.

I looked at the scarf in my hand, the scarf I had carried to the fence for the third time today. Suddenly I couldn't bear looking at that scarf again. I rolled it into a ball and tossed it with all my might, so that it sailed high across both fences and landed at the girl's feet.

She looked at me in surprise. She bent down and picked up the scarf and held it against her face. For a moment she smiled, the first smile I had seen on her face. Then she turned and walked away, slowly, without another word.

I looked after her but I didn't really see her or the fences that separated us. Instead I saw another fence — and Ruthie and Piet holding each other and loving each other on the heath in Westerbork. Ruthie and Piet! They ought to have gotten married and loved each other and had lots of red-haired children with blue eyes and heart-shaped faces. Instead they'd had three or

187

four horrible days and nights together in a dark and stinking cattle car and now Ruthie was dead — dead all alone on the bare floor of a drafty tent. And only God knew where Piet was.

I pictured the death cart, rumbling out of the camp with Ruthie's body piled in among all the other corpses. Nobody even to walk behind it to mourn for a last time. She was gone, her ashes mingled with those of the others, no privacy even in death.

I bent over heaving, vomiting violently where I stood.

Chapter 16

AT NIGHT, I kept seeing Ruthie pressing against the fence, calling for me. And the sweater — I kept seeing that too, hanging on the wires, trapped, caught, as I was. And I'd wake up in a sweat and with my cheeks wet with tears.

But this was only the beginning of that winter. One day we learned that we would have to move.

For about a week the convict laborers had been working feverishly around the clock to erect several rows of huge new barracks on the mustering square. Every other activity in the camp had stopped. There were no more labor squads, no more counting roll calls. And nobody knew what it all meant.

We watched the progress on the new barracks curiously. They were really not new at all, but old, weatherbeaten barracks that had been torn down somewhere else and reassembled here. We guessed that they might have come from Poland — just like the tent camp women.

As long as we kept our distance, the workmen didn't interfere with our watching, but the minute someone tried to move too close, the *kapos* rushed in with their clubs swinging. The *kapos* were the convict foremen, hardened criminals who had been entrusted with keeping order in our camp. The Germans themselves rarely showed their faces inside the camp these days. Even Red Müller and Lübke, the two most fanatical of the SS men, now seldom approached closer than the main gate. Rumor had it that the Germans were worried that they might catch the typhus fever now rampant in the camp. Some people thought this was the reason too why the work squads had been abolished. We had been put into a quarantine of sorts.

As moving day approached, more news filtered into the camp. We were told that we would have to crowd even closer together in our new quarters. There'd be fewer barracks for us because space was needed for the tent camp women. They would be moved into our old barracks. Everything was being rushed to get them out of the tents before the weather turned any colder. That made sense. It seemed doubtful that any of the tent camp women would be able to survive the first snowfall.

Still, it was hard to believe that our new quarters could be even more cramped than what we were living in now. We had made room for additional people several times already. The bar-racks day rooms had long ago been filled with bunk beds and the double-decker bunks had been replaced by triple-decker ones. How many more people could one fit into a given space?

Finally moving day came. With our bundles of possessions we trudged through the opening in the new fence that now would separate us from our old quarters. The new buildings looked curiously unfinished, partly because of the deep, open trenches that had been dug around each one of them.

"Those are probably to bury us in," someone joked, a grim sort of joke. Nobody laughed. It could too easily come true.

Inside, we stared in disbelief. At first glance it looked as if the huge shed had been solidly filled with bunks. There didn't seem to be any spaces between them. But eventually the pattern emerged. The bunks had been grouped together in blocks of twelve, three bunks deep and four bunks wide. And only very narrow aisles had been left between those solid blocks.

Our new barracks leader was standing in the doorway, crossing off names on her list.

"Find beds for yourselves," she kept repeating as people streamed in past her. "Just remember, you'll have to sleep two to a bed."

Two to a bed! I did some rapid arithmetic. That meant that each of those groups of triple-decker bunks would have to sleep seventy-two people. It hardly seemed possible.

We looked around for familiar faces but

somehow everybody we knew seemed to have been dispersed.

"We'd better concentrate on finding a decent bunk," my mother said, gently pushing me ahead of her down the aisle. After some looking, we were lucky enough to find an empty top bunk on the outside and I climbed up quickly to claim our find. For people limber enough to climb to that height, top bunks were the best. You had more light and more air up there and you could sit up and move around at will.

Slowly the beds filled up. From our high perch, my mother spotted a friend who had worked with her in one of the work squads, and she waved her over to claim the bunk next to us. Ollie was in her late twenties. She would share her bed with her elderly mother. Since the only access to their bed was across our bunk, we were glad to have found neighbors we knew and liked.

It didn't take us long to get organized. Everything we owned went under the mattress. The blankets went on top. Afterwards we just sat there, trying to adjust to the new situation. The outlook was pretty grim. Having seen the tent camp women, we knew that the bottom of the hill was still a good ways down. But the trend was definitely downhill.

Later my mother went to see how my father had fared. With all the confusion there was no problem about getting into one of the men's barracks. She found him resting in a lower bunk he shared with a Westerbork friend. My father spent most of his time resting now. He had been very much weakened by all his illnesses.

Too restless and worried to sit around while she was gone, I climbed down to do some investigating of my own. I hoped to find some of our old friends. After a while I spotted Sarah several bunk blocks down the aisle. She and her older sister shared an outside lower bunk while their mother was next to them, sharing an inside lower bunk with a stranger. There were certain advantages to having a lower bunk too. It was easier to get to, old people and small children ran fewer risks of falling, and you could stow your gear under the bed.

The people unlucky enough to draw middle bunks had no advantages at all. Only very small children could sit up straight in a middle bunk. Adults had the choice of either lying down or getting out of bed and hanging around in the aisles. After we had been settled in the new barracks for a few days it became clear that the people we saw milling about or eating their supper standing up while leaning against a bunk were the hapless owners of middle bunks.

My mother and I found that we had been lucky in drawing Ollie as a bunk mate. She was cheerful, resourceful, and sensible. She and her husband had both been journalists in Prague before the war and she was full of stories about their adventures. Most of her stories were hilariously funny because she saw things in a funny light. And they were liberally laced with invectives and four-letter words delivered in a strong and rather droll Czech accent. The bad language made my mother squirm uncomfortably because of my presence but it delighted me no end. Ollie treated me like an equal and not a child. In her presence I felt sophisticated and mature.

It was Ollie who started the great bug hunt. The new barracks literally crawled with bugs. Big black bedbugs lived in the cracks of the wooden beds and probably in the walls and floor-boards too. Lice inhabited the stained old straw mattresses. At night both kinds of vermin crawled out of their hiding places to feast on our blood. In the daytime they were invisible, safely hidden out of reach.

"This calls for psychological warfare," Ollie declared. "You've got to catch them when they don't expect you."

Ollie did it with a flashlight, an ancient hand-generated one that didn't need any batteries. Shortly after the lights went out at night, Ollie started pumping her flashlight under her blankets to cut down on the noise. Then, with a sudden sweeping motion, she'd shine it on the edge of the bed. Sure enough, invariably she caught at least two or three of the little pests out in the open, trapped in the beam of her light. Those bedbugs were so fat and overfed that they couldn't even run fast to escape. With lightning speed Ollie would swoop down on the hapless insect and scoop it up into a little jar she kept for just that purpose. After a few tries she usually had five or six prisoners safely stowed away and secured with the screw-on top. Then we'd go to sleep, satisfied that we'd done something to thwart our adversaries. It was all nonsense of course — there were hundreds more where those few bugs came from and our forays hardly made a dent. But in the morning Ollie carried her jar triumphantly to be emptied and flushed down the washroom toilet, if the toilet happened to be operative that day. It was the only sensible way to get rid of bedbugs. Their hard black shells made them terribly hard to kill.

The clothing lice were easier to kill but harder to find. They were tiny and almost totally color-less — transparent particles clinging to the seams of our clothes. We made it a ritual to look for them before we put on our clothes in the morning, carefully searching each seam and then squashing the offending insects between our fingernails. It made a satisfying, popping sound.

"Monkey business," Ollie called it.

"That's right! I feel like I'm in a zoo anyway," I said with a laugh. But the image lingered with me. A cage full of nitpicking monkeys squeezed into our cage — chattering away at each other, caching our morsels of food. Was that what we looked like to others?

The comparison with the monkeys was even more striking when we began to check each other's hair for lice. This was the one kind of vermin I dreaded most. I still remembered viv-idly how squeamish I had felt about the tur-baned women and children in Westerbork who had been treated for lice in their hair. My own hair had grown all the way to my shoulders again since that long-ago day in Amsterdam when Mr. Hemelrijk had cut it before I went to the camp. All through the years in Westerbork and also here in Belsen I had taken great care to keep my hair very clean. But now, one morning, my mother discovered the tell-tale signs. You couldn't see hair lice — they were too small. But you could see their eggs — tiny gray blobs, each carefully wrapped around an individual hair. Those eggs couldn't be washed away or combed out. The only cure was either cutting the hair down to the scalp or treating it with a very strong antiseptic.

I think my mother knew how I felt about cutting my hair.

"Let's ask Madame Sophia if she can help us," she said. "She may still have some of that strong stuff she kept in that mysterious bottle of hers. Perhaps she'll trade us a hair treatment for something else."

Madame Sophia was one of the Greek ladies. I think the mysterious disinfectant she hoarded in a big brown bottle was Lysol, but it might have been something else. Anyway, for a time in the old barracks, Madame Sophia had been very much in business with her potent concoction. Hair lice had been a problem in the camp all along.

It wasn't easy to find Madame Sophia among the five hundred women in the new barracks — even the Greeks had been scattered during the move. But we finally found her, tucked away in a far corner, and she agreed to undertake the operation in return for some woolen gloves. She gave us instructions as to what we would need. A towel, some soap, some kind of cotton scarf.

She herself went to see if she could warm up some water on top of the one little iron stove in the center of the big barracks.

We met her a little later in the washroom. We had to wait to get to a free faucet — there was never enough water for all the people. While I leaned over the iron sink, Madame Sophia carefully poured some of the stuff from her precious bottle into my hair.

"Rub," she told my mother. "Rub hard."

My mother rubbed and rinsed under the watchful eye of Madame Sophia, carefully husbanding the little bit of tepid water from Madame Sophia's bowl. She rinsed some more with cold water, making me yelp from the sudden shock of it. Then she wrapped the towel around my head.

"I hope you don't catch your death sitting around in the cold with wet hair," she sighed.

Madame Sophia ran the fine end of my comb through my hair. She inspected the comb carefully.

"I think we did it," she said. "The eggs are combing out. It's strong stuff, this antiseptic in my bottle!"

I wrapped the scarf around my head, partly to keep warm, partly to protect my hair from fresh contamination. I promised myself to keep my hair covered from now on.

The days dragged on, each one exactly like the last. There just was nothing to do and no place to go. Outside it was snowing on and off, filling the trenches and turning the paths into ankle-deep mud. Going to the latrine became an expedition.

My mother kept busy because my father was sick again with another bout of camp fever. He was more or less permanently in bed by now, too weak to move around very much. My mother went to see him often, to check if he'd gotten his food or to bring him some water in the green metal water bottle we had brought with us from Westerbork. To get water she would get up very early — before dawn, really — to stand in line at the one decent water faucet we still had in the camp, near the big gate. All the washroom faucets only trickled a little rusty water by now and the water pressure seemed to get lower day by day. So my mother made the trip to the good faucet twice each morning, first for my father and then again for herself and for me. I don't know how she kept going. It took such an effort just to live through each day. I myself seemed to be sinking rapidly into feverish lethargy.

On New Year's Eve we recklessly opened our last can of sardines. My father even got up to come and share it with us.

"Now it's camp rations forever," my mother sighed, as if we had regularly feasted on such delicacies all along.

"It can't be long anymore," my father said. "We know the Russians are advancing. We know that from the tent camp women."

"And the Germans are in such a bad temper — the war must be going badly for them," I said.

"Perhaps we'll even be exchanged after all," my mother said dreamily.

My father and I smiled at each other behind her back. Exchange for Germans in South America had been our hope and dream when we first came to Belsen. Now almost a year had passed. But my mother had always clung stubbornly to her hopes.

Nineteen forty-five started out just as badly as 1944 had ended. It seemed awful to look forward to a whole new year. This was the third New Year's Day I had spent in a prison camp and time seemed to stretch out eternally before me. I didn't even want to listen to the hopeful rumors about the advancing Russian army. For three long years I had hoped and hoped and I was tired of dreaming.

The only thing I wanted to do right now was to sit on my bunk with my notebook and pencil, filling pages and pages with sketches and poems and scribbled diary notes. It was still the same ordinary school copybook I had brought with me from Holland. I was getting to the last few pages and I dreaded the moment when I wouldn't have any paper left on which to record my thoughts. Making up poems and writing them down was a way of escaping — an escape no amount of fencing or guard towers could prevent. Sitting on my half of that top bunk in the crowded barracks — on top of and surrounded by all my worldly possessions — I escaped to far-away places where the world was still wide open and beautiful and where nothing ugly could touch me at all.

And then I too came down with the camp fever. It started with cramps and chills and chattering teeth during the night and by morning I could hardly get down from the bunk for the trip to the washroom.

Now my mother had two patients on her hands. She had a touch of the illness herself — almost everybody in camp did — but she ignored it most of the time because my father and I needed her help.

I stayed in bed, drowsing when the fever was high, sitting up when I felt a little better. My mother brought me my bowl of soup each day but now I wasn't even hungry — the smell of the turnips made me want to throw up. The only thing I wanted to do was scribble in my notebook. I wrote about rolling wheat fields — the ones I remembered from my childhood summers — and about shady trees and a calm blue sea under a starry sky. Perhaps it was the fever that brought on these fantasies, or perhaps it was just my strong need to blot out everything that was so unbearably ugly in the real world around me.

I thought of death during those days of illness on my top bunk. Why should anyone be afraid of death, I wondered. Weren't we dying anyway . . . bit by bit . . . a slow death by starvation? Dying was so much easier than living, the way things were now. I could easily imagine lying back and closing my eyes and sleeping away into death — like Ruthie. What was hard was to keep on doing all the things that kept you from dying — the daily routines that kept you alive. What would Grannie say now, I wondered. Would she still think that life was an adventure and interesting?

And then I felt guilty about my thoughts. Of course Grannie would tell me to go on struggling, just as my parents were struggling to live for each other and for me. As long as there was still the slightest chance for liberation each of us had to fight to survive.

One night I woke up from a nightmarish dream, my mouth dry, the blood pulsing painfully against my temples. Next to me my mother was asleep in her half of the bunk, the blanket drawn about her, her arm protectively thrown around me. She was as close as anyone could be, but I felt oddly alone, alone among all these hundreds of sleeping women. I heard them breathing and rustling around, but I still felt apart from them — separated.

All alone in my monkey cage. The image came back to me again. And suddenly I felt angry and sad and terrified all at once. Then I found myself praying, not the childish prayers I had been taught when I was young, or the ritual prayers I had tried so hard to learn when Lewis had tried to make a good Jew out of me. It was a different kind of prayer, a wordless communicating with something larger than I and yet deep within myself. These feelings surprised me because of late I had doubted the existence of God.

A just God wouldn't let all the unjust things happen to us! No matter what Sarah said.

Oh, but I wanted Sarah to be right. I wanted to believe — desperately. Time was running out. The moment had come for God to produce a miracle.

You must let something happen now, God, I prayed defiantly. If you mean for me to go on living, it's up to You now!

Suddenly, in the midst of my rebelling, I felt wonderfully calm. Something would happen soon, I was sure of it now. One way or another.

I lay back and closed my eyes, giving myself to the temporary escape of sleep. I slept well that night, and deeply, and without dreams. And when something tugged at my consciousness to wake me up, I fought against opening my eyes and coming back to reality.

But the tugging was physical and it continued. I half opened my eyes and I saw my mother's face, hovering over the edge of the bed. She was fully dressed and she was balanced on the middle bunk, pulling at my shoulders to wake me up.

"Wake up, wake up, Rosemarie," she said urgently. "You've got to wake up and get dressed. It's very important. There is no time to be lost."

Chapter 17

I STRUGGLED UP, too drowsy to understand what my mother was saying to me. Next to me, Ollie too sat up in her bed.

"Are you out of your mind, Louise?" she asked. "This child is running a fever."

"The Exchange Commission is here," my mother said. "They are finally really here. They want to see everyone with South American passports."

"How do you know?" I asked, reaching for my ski pants.

"I saw them. A whole group of them. High brass, with lots of gold braid on the caps and medals pinned to their chests. They are setting up some kind of office in the infirmary."

"But why does Rosie have to go?" Ollie asked. "I mean — couldn't you explain that she is sick right now? You could always show them her passport."

My mother shook her head.

"No. Rosemarie must come. I don't know why exactly — it's just a feeling. I think we should show up together before the commissioners."

She turned to me again.

"Hurry up, Rosie. I've called your father too and he'll meet us over there. If we get there before the general announcement is made we may not have to wait in line so long."

With Ollie still shaking her head, I pulled on my sweater and began to lace up my boots. My mother helped me down from the bed. My knees were shaky and I felt a bit dizzy after so much time in bed.

My mother fussed over me, adjusting my scarf, pulling the folds high up over my chin.

"Do you have your gloves?" she asked, as if I were a five-year-old going out for a walk in the park. "All right, then let's go. Put your hands in your pockets to keep warm."

Outside the door of the barracks I gasped as the fresh cold air rushed into my lungs. After so many days of breathing the spent, smelly barracks fumes, the clean outside air was almost too pure for me. It made my head spin.

I leaned on my mother as we made our way to the infirmary. It was just two barracks away, but the way seemed interminable. Such an effort — just moving one foot before the other. Would I make it? But I mustn't let my mother see how hard it was for me. She had enough to worry about.

At the infirmary, people were lined up already, waiting to be interviewed. My father was there too. I hadn't seen him for days and I was shocked to note the change in him. He seemed to have shrunk — even his black cap looked too big on him now, the way it hung down halfway to his eyes. Below it, his face looked even narrower and paler. And there were deep lines etched around his eyes and along his cheeks.

He bent down to kiss me, pulling me into the line. He tried hard to pretend that he was feeling fine, but I could see that he was very weak. Every once in a while, when he thought that my mother and I weren't looking at him, he would momentarily rest by leaning against the wall.

The line moved forward slowly. Behind us it grew rapidly as the word about the commission spread through the camp. Finally it was our turn. Four high-ranking SS officers and one civilian sat behind the table in the small makeshift office, leafing through stacks of lists and other important papers. They looked us over searchingly before they accepted our proffered passports, and almost mechanically I stood a little taller and pulled my shoulders back. They took a long time studying the passports and comparing our names to the names on their lists. Red Müller was in the room, fawning over the commission members and glaring at us now and then. Seeing him made me remember that incident of the missing needles and I hoped that he wouldn't notice me.

The civilian was the spokesman for the group.

"Brenner — Charles, Louise, Rosemarie," he read off the list. He turned to us.

"Are all three of you ready and prepared to

leave on this exchange transport early tomorrow morning?" he asked.

"Yes, sir, we certainly are," my mother said clearly.

"Then report to the main gate with your belongings at seven tomorrow morning. We'll leave promptly then. Next?"

We had been dismissed.

"Thank God, we made it," my mother said outside. She looked like a new person. Her face was animated and she walked with a new spring in her step. I wished I could feel as excited as she did. But somehow I felt numb inside.

It can't be true anyway, I told myself. It's a trick. They won't really let us go.

I wouldn't let myself get excited. I didn't want to be disappointed in the end.

We walked on, past small knots of people who had been to see the commission before us and who were now discussing the results.

"Are you on the list?" a woman asked us. When my mother nodded, she smiled. "We too. But the Goldsteins before us were told they couldn't come along because two members of their family were sick in bed. They will take only people who are well enough to travel."

I looked at my mother. "How did you guess?" I whispered. My mother shrugged her shoulders.

"Just intuition," she said.

Back in the barracks my mother made me lie down and rest. "You'll need all your strength tomorrow," she declared. Ollie helped her pack. Ollie didn't have a South American passport. For her there was no chance to leave.

I was content to let Ollie do my share of the work. That way I didn't have to think about it. I was too tired to think, to wonder — too tired even to hope.

In the morning, when we left the bunk, Ollie embraced us. "Good luck," she whispered. "We'll get in touch after the war. Think of us when you're free. Where are they sending you anyway? Do you know?"

"Switzerland, I think," my mother said. "We are to be exchanged for Germans from South America. That's what I heard."

"Switzerland!" Ollie said dreamily. "I always loved the Swiss mountains. Say hello to the Alps for me."

"The war will be over soon," my mother said, clinging to Ollie. "Hold on until then."

I didn't say anything. The lump in my throat was too thick. Besides, what could you say to friends you were leaving behind in a place like this?

I hardly dared look back at Ollie. How would I feel if our roles were reversed? But of course, we were not really going to Switzerland. Maybe they were sending us somewhere even worse than Belsen. How could you believe what the Gestapo said?

In deep gloom I followed my parents to the camp gate.

While we waited I looked around to see who was coming with us. I spotted Sarah and her family and we waved to each other. It made me feel a little better to see a friend.

Suddenly I could hardly wait to get started.

Even if it was all a lie, at least something was happening now. We were leaving — we were actually leaving Belsen behind forever.

I quickened my step, as if my own hastened pace could hurry along the slowly moving column. We'll know when we get to the train, I thought. If it's cattle cars, I'll know that our future will not be better. My God, why is everyone moving so slowly. I can't wait to get to that train!

But I had to wait a little longer. We stopped at the bath house for a last shower, a final fumigation of our clothes. I fumed at the delay. It was unfair. It was unbearable!

Then we were given soup. Another delay! But the soup was rich and hot, thick with vegetables I hadn't remembered existed and even with bits of meat. I stared at the soup. Could it all be true after all? They wouldn't give us soup like this if they weren't actually sending us to freedom.

"Stop daydreaming and eat your soup," my mother said. I took a spoon and then another. Yes, the soup was real. Everything was real! We were going to Switzerland!

Everybody around me was gobbling the soup, eating with big, gulping bites, hardly noticing that the soup was terribly salty. Who cared about a little salt? Nothing mattered except that our stomachs were full.

Red Müller came into the hall, scowling at us.

"Hurry, hurry," he shouted. "If you want to leave, hurry up now. We can't use laggards. Let's get in line. Forward! March!"

"Just look at his face," my mother whispered. "He hates to see us escape from his clutches!"

We lined up for the walk.

"Are they going to make us carry everything all the way to the train?" I sighed. After the soup and the bath my legs felt like lead and I remembered the long walk when we came to Belsen. But then I saw the trucks, parked down the road. Everybody got to ride, this time.

The train was waiting for us at the station. A passenger train! Marked with the Red Cross insignia. There were even a few second-class compartments.

"Now I'm really beginning to believe it's all true," Sarah's mother said, echoing my thoughts. She and her family crowded into the same compartment with us.

Sarah's father shook his head. "I'll believe it when I arrive in Switzerland," he muttered.

"We are moving," Sarah burst out. "We are really leaving Belsen!" Everybody looked out of the window. It was true, the snowy platforms of the Celle station slowly receded from our view.

We were still busy stowing away our few possessions in the overhead racks when two men of our group, who had been designated transport leaders, came through the train to check on us.

"Great news! Take off your stars," they almost shouted. "The SS Commandant himself gave us the orders! All stars to be removed as soon as the train is on its way!"

Take off our stars! We looked at each other. Then it *was* true. It was really true. We would

209

be exchanged. We were traveling toward freedom!

We tore off the stars, not caring if we ripped holes in our clothes in the process. Below the stars, the outlines remained on our garments, etched there where the years of wear had faded the cloth around the wretched badges.

The train rumbled on, over mile after mile of snow-covered fields. Sarah and I stared out of the window, hungry for new sights, for a look at the outside world after such a long time behind barbed-wire fences. Everything seemed exciting, even just an old farmhouse or a shabby barn.

The thirst started a couple of hours later. Everybody began to feel it at about the same time. It was long past noon, but we were not really hungry. What we wanted was something to drink.

Sarah went to investigate. She came back, stricken. There was nothing to drink on the train. The water faucets at the ends of the cars were dry. There was no water on the train at all. And in all the compartments there were thirsty people. Terribly thirsty.

"It's that soup they gave us," my mother said. "Remember how salty it was? They probably did it on purpose. Red Müller's last act of revenge."

We all remembered the soup. We had gulped it down greedily, not even really noticing the saltiness, because the soup had been so thick and rich. And now we suffered. We suffered for hours. My tongue felt like leather — no, like cotton — sticking to the roof of my mouth. I tried to think about other things — to look out of the window, to count the telegraph poles flashing by. But even the snow made me think of water. Large glasses of water, clear and cold. And the more I thought of it, the drier I felt.

Late that evening the Germans finally brought some food and something to drink on board. We pounced on the drinks, spilling precious drops in our haste. But a sense of the terrible thirst lingered. A small cup of ersatz coffee couldn't erase the thirst.

It was an odd, erratic journey. The train stopped often — always on deserted stretches of track. Though we could move through the train at will, we couldn't get off, even when it was halted. The doors were locked and when someone opened a window and leaned out too far, an armed guard appeared immediately to wave him back. Even without our stars we were still very much prisoners.

Everywhere we passed bombed-out structures — factories in ruins, gasoline storage tanks leveled to the ground. The devastation amazed us. None of the news that had somehow filtered into the camps had prepared us to find Germany in such ruins. Those planes we had seen passing high over our camp had done their job well.

"Just look at that," my father said. "So much destruction — and the Gestapo had nothing better to do than to worry about a few Jews in their camps. They must be insane. Really insane!"

From time to time the air-raid sirens sounded in a town we were passing through and then the train would stop and our guards would disappear to take to the shelters. We remained on the tracks in our locked train, a perfect target. It felt odd, sitting there and hearing the bombs explode all around us. Some fell close enough to shake the train. We are trapped, I thought. We can't get out and run. Wouldn't the guards love that! They were probably hoping we'd get hit!

We zigzagged through Germany in a crazy-quilt pattern, taking days for a trip that shouldn't have taken more than one day. Bombed-out stretches of railroad track necessitated the enormous detours.

We even passed through Berlin one night, where we stopped at a deserted suburban station. Even here the devastation was great. Blocks of gutted apartment buildings flanked the station, with their shattered windows and broken doors exposing the empty insides. I looked at these hollow shells with an odd mixture of horror and satisfaction. It served them right, I thought. Oh, God, look at it! The Germans got what they deserved! And then I shivered at the thought of living through such a night of falling bombs.

Finally the train began to travel south at a steady pace. Sarah's father, who had traveled a great deal in Germany before the war, began to read off landmarks as the station signs flashed by.

"We are approaching Switzerland," he told us at last. "It isn't far now."

Switzerland! I could hardly sit still anymore. Other people felt that way too. Everybody wandered back and forth between the compartments, to compare notes, to point out how close we were.

When we stopped again, just beyond a small hamlet, Sarah's father was sure.

"That's the last stop before the Swiss border. I remember the name. I've traveled to Switzerland along this route before. The border can't be more than a mile or two away."

Two miles to freedom. I wanted to shout and cry and run around all at the same time. But my mother put a restraining hand on my arm.

"Calm down, Rosie," she said. "We'll have plenty of time to celebrate when we arrive."

The train moved again. I could hear the reluctant screeching of the wheels and the sound of the steam escaping from the engine and then I felt the forward pressure as we began to gather speed. We leaned across each other, craning our necks, straining for our first glimpse of Swiss soil.

The train stopped so suddenly — without any warning — that we all bumped into each other and the luggage tumbled from the racks. There was nothing to see outside. Nothing but snow-laden trees crowded together in a thick patch of woodland. What was going on? Was this the border? Was this Switzerland?

I barely noticed the movement when the train began to reverse, rolling backwards ever so gently, so that it took a few moments before I grasped that the landscape was now passing before our eyes in the wrong direction.

We sat frozen, in silence — not daring to speak or to voice our fears.

Then we were back in the tiny railroad station we had left so happily just a few moments before. German guards swarmed around the train.

"Get out, get out," they shouted. "Bring the things you've got with you in your compartments. Out of the train, everybody — line up here."

We obeyed, remembering how we had disembarked on another snowy station platform just about a year ago. We lined up, the way we had been taught in Belsen, forming the neat rows of five that were second nature to us by now. And then we waited.

The Gestapo officers were conferring with our transport leaders. They gesticulated wildly, pointing to the lists in their hands, to the train, to the rest of us waiting in the shadows.

Finally the transport leaders approached.

"There aren't enough Germans waiting to be exchanged on the Swiss side of the border," they reported. "Some of you will have to stay behind. Here is the list of the people chosen to stay."

He called the names slowly, waiting each time for an acknowledgment. I heard the gasps and moans as the people responded to their names and stepped aside, out of the line. I held my breath, willing our name to be skipped, praying it would not be called. The names were called in no particular order, so there was no moment of safety, no point of respite. Inside my pockets

I crossed my fingers, as if that childish gesture could hold off the moment of doom.

I heard Sarah's name called and while I turned around to catch her eye — to see her reaction — I almost missed the calling of our own. My mother tugged at my sleeve and pulled me from the line. We were among the last to be called. It was the end of the list.

"Everybody else, back on the train," the SS officers shouted. Numbly I watched the other people, the lucky ones, climbing back on the train. Through the windows I saw them getting settled in their compartments again, putting their belongings back on the luggage racks. Someone opened a window and threw down a package that belonged to the woman standing on the platform next to me. It burst open, spilling sweaters and shoes into the snow. She retrieved it, clutching it as if it were a lost child, tears running down her cheeks.

Then the train moved — slowly, then faster and faster — people leaning out of open windows, waving good-bye to us. Good-bye! Hope sped away. Then it was only a blur, a black blur, trailing a cloud of white smoke down the track, rushing, rushing, toward Switzerland.

Biberach

1945

Chapter 18

I SUPPOSE it was the fever, because later on I hardly remembered anything that had happened after I saw that train rounding the bend. There were snatches of memories, bits of scenes that came back to me in time, but it was all very hazy and confused.

I remember sitting down on my rucksack because my legs just wouldn't hold me anymore. All I could think of was that they'd send us back now — back to Belsen — and I just couldn't bear the thought.

I don't know how long we waited there in that station, but it must have been many hours because the next thing I remember is that it was dark and it had started to snow. Thick flakes swirling in the cones of lamplight.

And then we were walking through the deserted streets of a little town. There were real houses with chinks of light seeping out around blackout curtains and once in a while a passerby stopped to stare at our ragged group. They didn't stop long, though, when they noticed the Gestapo officers who escorted us. Then they'd just melt away into the darkness.

It wasn't a long walk. Suddenly we had arrived. We entered a building four or five stories high. My knees buckled under me as we struggled up an immense stairway, or perhaps it just seemed so tall and broad because it was so hard for me to climb. My final memory is of a bed, a double decker too, but with a real mattress and a pillow in a clean pillow case. I recall the clean smell of that pillow case, but I don't remember how I got into bed, or if I undressed or just slept in my clothes. I slept, and if I had feverish dreams, I don't remember those either.

Three days later I was up and on my feet again, my knees still shaking like jelly but my mind clear enough again to wonder what I had missed.

My mother filled me in. We were in an army barracks, and the army commander had been fighting for three days with the Gestapo about what they would do with us. The Gestapo wanted to send us back to Belsen, but the army people kept saying that they had no trains to spare. Meanwhile half of our little group had collapsed — with fatigue, with diarrhea, with soaring fevers. At least three people had died the first night after gobbling down bowls full of a deliciously rich pea soup and bread. Starving stomachs cannot handle too much richness all at once.

Now a decision had been made. We were to be sent to a nearby camp for civilian internees, a camp under the supervision of the International Red Cross.

I didn't really care where we were going now, as long as it wasn't back to Belsen. The shock of having been taken from the train so close to the Swiss border still hadn't worn off. I thought I'd never care about anything again. I felt numb and empty.

My father came in with the news that we would leave tonight. Had he shriveled up more since I'd seen him last? It was hard to tell. I went through the motions of helping my mother re-pack our rucksacks again, but my mind wasn't on my work and I moved so slowly that she finally chased me away.

I went to the window and looked down on the traffic moving through the streets four stories below. It was odd, seeing a real town again, watching cars and trucks and people bound on their ordinary daily errands. Would I ever walk the streets of a city or town again — going home to a real house with furniture and belongings? When I closed my eyes I could see our house in Amsterdam, the living room with its red rug and the soft velvet pillows on the sofa. I almost could smell the cookies Grannie was baking in the kitchen, and then I remembered that Grannie was dead and our furniture was gone and nothing would ever be quite the same.

It was dusk when we were finally told to get ready, a quiet hour when few civilians would be around to see us being taken away. We traveled again by train, and by truck. The distance was short but it was night when we arrived at our destination and it was hard to see anything.

The large shape of a building loomed out of the darkness, like a ship drifting in from a fog. Light streamed out of an open door through which we were ushered into a huge room, a ballroom really, with mirrors on the walls and crystal chandeliers swinging from high ceilings. But the polished parquet floor was covered with heaps of straw, large mounds of it piled against the walls on either side of the room.

We were to sleep here, we were told, on the straw. Tomorrow we would be processed into the camp proper.

It was a wretched night. I spread my blankets on the straw and tried to sleep, but the coarse stalks poked through the blankets, sticking me whenever I tried to move. This was even worse than the lumpy straw mattresses in Belsen. Or had three nights on the soft beds in the army barracks spoiled me?

By morning I itched all over, and I felt stiff and sore. What now, I wondered. What are they going to do with us next?

We didn't have long to wait. Just after daybreak a great stir and motion engulfed us — purposeful people coming in, setting up tables, arranging file folders and cards. The English people who had been interned in this camp for more than four years were getting ready to welcome us into their midst.

They can't be happy about it, I thought, as I inched along in the line toward the registration table. Would I welcome such a squalid crew of half-starved strangers? In the morning light, with bright sunshine streaming in through tall French windows, our little group looked even more weary and bedraggled than before. And indeed the faces of the English camp officials reflected a mixture of pity and disgust.

I hadn't counted on having to be checked for lice and other vermin — not right away, before they'd even let us into the new camp. But several young nurses were ready and waiting for us, and they were firm about what they had to do. The words were in English and I understood only a few phrases here and there, but the meaning was clear. Bugs were not tolerated at camp Biberach.

I was quite confident that my hair was clean. After all, I'd had it treated by Madame Sophia just a few weeks ago, and I had faithfully kept it covered ever since then. So I didn't worry at all when I sat down to let the English nurse look through my hair.

She combed through it and then she said something to me which I didn't quite understand, so I just smiled and started to get up, thinking I'd been dismissed. But she held me down, with a slight pressure of her hand on my shoulder, and then I saw that she had a pair of scissors in her hand.

"Oh, no! Please don't cut my hair!" I said it with such anguish that she too understood what I'd said, despite the language barrier. She hesitated for a moment, her face troubled. But then she shook her head.

"I've got to do it," she said gently. "You do have vermin in your hair. We can't have the rest of the camp infected. Your hair will grow again."

I sat still, feeling the cold metal of the scissors against my scalp, hearing the quick click-click of metal against metal. There was no mirror, thank God. But I saw the chunks of brown hair falling on my lap and sliding to the floor and I remembered again Amsterdam and Mr. Hemelrijk's makeshift beauty parlor. I felt my nails digging into my palms. I'm not going to cry, I thought — I'm not going to cry!

When she was finished with me I ran my hand through my hair. It felt terribly short and bare. I tried to pull it forward but I couldn't. There wasn't even enough left to cover my ears.

"It will grow quickly, Rosemarie," my mother comforted. "And it really looks quite nice, the way it is now. It's all curly at the ends. It makes your face look a lot fuller too."

I was so upset about my hair that I didn't even wonder what our new quarters would be like. But when I finally saw them, the surprise almost made me forget about the haircut. The English people had quickly cleared out two barracks for us, but what they called barracks was a far cry from what we had known before. They were grand! These barracks were built of stone and they were divided into rooms of different sizes, sleeping anywhere from two to six people. And the washrooms and toilets had doors!

Our two barracks were separated from the rest of the camp with a wire-mesh fence. We were to be kept in quarantine for a few weeks, until the sick among us got better and the camp doctor had had a chance to check us and treat whatever he could treat. He was a very young man — he couldn't have been out of medical school for very long when he was interned — and I think our group with all our various ailments must have been a challenge to him.

"Any day now we'll be able to give you Red Cross packages," he told us. "Just like we get every two weeks."

Right now they were doling out the food in our packages to us in small doses, putting some of it into the daily vegetable soup supplied by the German camp kitchen. Each day we got a little more — some cheese, some chocolate, a bit of meat. The doctor was afraid that we might all die if we were given too rich a diet too suddenly. I knew what he meant. We all remembered the people who had died after eating the rich pea soup in the Ravensburg army barracks.

And still, those little extras hadn't prepared us for the thrill of holding a whole Red Cross package in our hands. Was all of this for me? I rummaged through the box, barely believing my eyes. Such treasures! Cans of butter, powdered egg yolk, chocolate bars, condensed milk. Who could ask for anything more?

Each package had to last two weeks — extra food to add to our ordinary camp rations. I even thought the regular camp soup was delicious, to the surprise of the English people, who couldn't stand it anymore after eating it for four years as a steady diet. With the extras from the Red Cross packages, each meal became a feast.

One day I walked into Sarah's room and found her eating a piece of bread heavily loaded with bacon. The bacon came rolled up in round cans and was really meant to be fried. But since we had no cooking facilities, we ate it uncooked, from the can. It was terribly greasy, yet we all craved fat because that was something we had lacked for years in our diets.

I was surprised to see Sarah eating the bacon. Her family was so staunchly orthodox in their religious observances, it seemed odd to see her eating pork. Obviously they had not been able to adhere to their kosher practices in the camps. But bacon! I wondered what Sarah's pious father would say about that.

Sarah seemed to guess my thoughts, because she suddenly blushed.

"My father said I should eat this bacon," she said defensively. "He's decided it's important for me to eat as much fat as possible right now and it's the only kind to be had."

The English people in camp Biberach shared

more than just their Red Cross packages with us. One day a lady came into our quarantine compound to measure all of the children for new shoes. She had brought the shoes with her from the Red Cross storage shed: shiny brown oxfords in assorted sizes.

Shoes! I couldn't wait to get new shoes!

I lined up with the others, but when it was my turn, the nice gray-haired lady shook her head.

"You're sixteen, aren't you, dear?" she asked, checking her list. "I'm afraid you are too old for shoes. They are only for children fifteen or under."

"But I need shoes," I pleaded. "Look, my ski boots are all torn and they are much too small for me now."

The lady looked and she agreed that I did need new shoes very badly indeed, but unfortunately there were no ladies' shoes in the Red Cross storehouse.

"But my feet are small," I argued. "I can wear children's sizes. My feet are smaller than Sarah's. Sarah is getting shoes and she is only a few months younger than I!"

But the lady was adamant. Rules were rules. She couldn't give me children's shoes. I was above the age.

"You're not a child anymore," she said kindly, with the sort of smile meant to encourage me. "You are a young lady now."

I knew she meant well, but I was heartbroken. She could see it in my face and she looked troubled.

"Perhaps I can find some shoes for you," she said. "I'll look around."

I kept my composure until I got back to our room. But when I saw my mother, I couldn't hold back anymore. The tears came — the tears I hadn't shed when Grannie died, or Ruthie. Now I cried — hot, wet tears — because of a pair of shoes! I knew it was silly while I cried, and I told my mother so, between sobs, but I couldn't stop the tears.

My mother sat down and cradled my head in her lap.

"Go on crying, Rosie," she said. "It's a good thing to be able to cry about little things. It is a healing process."

The lady kept her word and brought me some shoes the next day. It hadn't been easy to find someone with feet as small as mine — and someone who could spare some shoes. But an old lady had given her a pair she didn't need and she brought them to me proudly.

I stared at the shoes. When had people worn a style like that? Back in the 1920's, I guessed. They were high-heeled beige pumps with a strap across the instep and sharply pointed toes. I put them on and they looked grotesque over my ankle socks. I had never worn high heels before, so I wobbled and teetered as I walked around, trying them on.

"Oh, they fit fine," the lady said, looking pleased. Somehow I managed to mumble my thanks, not as graciously as she deserved. Inwardly I still felt like crying. I'd have to wear those awful shoes because they were better than my torn ski boots and there was nothing else. But I still resented the fact that I was too old for the shiny oxfords.

"A young lady," my benefactor had called me. "You're not a child anymore."

I wasn't a child any longer—that was true. But how was I supposed to act? In Belsen it was safer to be a child. . . . I was kept from growing up, from seeming my age, even when I wanted to. And now? How could I learn to grow up overnight?

Chapter 19

FINALLY, after several weeks, our quarantine was lifted and we were able to explore the rest of the camp. Camp Biberach, I discovered, was built on what must have been the grounds and gardens of a lovely baroque country estate. The large building where we had spent our first night was the main house, which the Gestapo had taken over as an administration building. In spite of its new military purpose, the main building still looked elegant with dormer windows and curved roofs and large French doors opening on wide terraces.

The big building was also used as a school building for the children in the camp. Each morning the teacher assembled his small group of school-age youngsters at the fence separating us from the big house, and a guard would open the gate and let them file into the schoolrooms assigned to them.

After our quarantine was lifted, the children in our group were invited to join the little school. And this time, luckily, I was not considered too old!

"Of course you may come," the English schoolmaster said. "We'd like all of you to learn English as quickly as possible."

In the schoolroom we were given bright, colorful American second- and third-grade readers. Like our food packages, they had been supplied by the Red Cross. I leafed through the pages, looking at the illustrations. A boy, a girl, a dog, romping through the neat streets of a little town — green lawns, picket fences, white clapboard houses. Was there really such a place? Did a peaceful and happy town like that exist somewhere in far-off America?

What bliss to hold a book in my hands again! The only English words I knew were a half dozen Mother Goose nursery rhymes I had learned long ago in school. What could you do with the vocabulary found in "Baa Baa Black Sheep"? But if you were as starved for something to read as I was, you found a way. I just read and read the foreign words, and suddenly they began to have meaning. I absorbed the English language almost by osmosis.

I think the English people in the camp were surprised at how content we all were with the conditions in Camp Biberach. They had been here four years, ever since the German army had captured the tiny Channel Islands of Jersey and

Guernsey and had carried off all the people who were not native-born islanders. Many of them were retired teachers and civil servants who had settled on the islands for quiet retirement years. Little had they known what was in store for them!

All those years the English prisoners had followed the slow, agonizing course of the war on a carefully hidden shortwave radio set. In spite of their fears that the Germans might catch them at it, the men went to listen to the BBC religiously twice a day. The penalties they risked were harsh, but the people in the camp lived for their daily dose of news. It made them feel they were still part of the world.

And now, at least, the news was almost always good. On all fronts the Allies were advancing. In Italy, in France, the Russians from the East. Not fast enough, of course. Not fast enough for people waiting to be liberated.

I listened to people discussing the daily reports but there was no sense of urgency in me anymore. I was content to know that the end of the war was approaching, but I didn't count the days. This was a time of rest and healing for me, a timeless limbo in which I could slowly learn to live again. Day by day I gained weight and strength and my hair grew inch by inch. When I looked in the bathroom mirror I no longer faced a scarecrow. My face was growing rounder and my body filled out and I noticed that curves were beginning to appear in the right places. I *was* growing up.

And when my mother said to me one morning in March, "Well, Rosemarie, it really looks as if we might be free for your next birthday," I thought, yes, it might be so — this time it might be so.

The war truly drew closer. People pored over clandestine maps, pinpointing the movements of the French, the British, the American armies. Who would reach us first? It was almost like a race.

At night we could hear the bombardments of nearby cities. Each night the bombs seemed to be falling on nearer and nearer targets. The ground shook and the windows rattled. I ran to the window. In the east the sky had turned a fiery red. It must be Ulm, the cathedral town, going up in flames. I couldn't sleep. All night long I watched the red glow until the rising sun competed with the fierce conflagration.

The next day German refugees by the hundreds streamed down the road from Ulm which ran right past our camp. They came on bicycles and in trucks, or on foot, dragging handcarts with their belongings behind them. For hours they drifted past, scarcely glancing at where we stood behind our fences, watching them.

Later, groups of young men in makeshift uniforms marched in the opposite direction. Some carried rifles, others just sticks and clubs.

"That's the Heimwehr," my mother said, "the local militia. Look, they are wearing Hitler Youth armbands. Why, some of them are only boys. Are these the troops that are supposed to stop the Allied armies? Can't they see what is coming? Why don't they just give up?"

233

I couldn't leave the fence. There was too much going on. All morning the guns kept on booming. The noise was moving closer and closer all the time. What was happening? Outside our camp gates the Gestapo guards rushed around madly, nervously loading files and pieces of furniture into army trucks. A box of papers fell, scattering its contents. It was ignored. The pieces of paper fluttered to the ground, got snagged on the fence, festooned the bushes. We stood and watched the guards but now, finally, they hardly noticed us. Like the fleeing civilians, they were concerned only with getting away.

"It has to be the Allies," my father said after a specially loud cannon blast. "I hope they know there is a prison camp here. I think we're right in the path of the advancing army."

He had hardly spoken when there was a deafening volley of shots. It made the windowpanes rattle all around us.

"Hey, they're shooting at us!" someone yelled. "There are Allied tanks out there. They hit the Red Cross storage shed. It's on fire!"

Our Red Cross packages! They were too precious to be lost. Some of the men went dashing to the shed. What would they do? Beat out the flames with their bare hands? But you couldn't just stand by and watch them burn.

There was another volley of shots. Then, loud and clear, came a woman's voice. "They are here! They are here! The liberators are here!"

I couldn't see who had shouted it, but her words made my spine tingle. The liberators! Of course, that's what they were!

"Come on, let's show them we are friends," the woman yelled again. "Wave something white — a handkerchief, a scarf, anything. Show them we are here."

The crowd began moving. Faster and faster. We all began to run toward the fence that separated the camp from the potato fields beyond. I ran too, swept along by the crowd. I searched my pocket for a handkerchief — for anything — just something to wave. It didn't occur to me or anyone else that the Allied bullets might hurt us, too.

By the time I reached the fence, the fire was out in the Red Cross shed. The damage was small. The outside wall was charred on one side. That was all.

Outside the fence the tanks that had inflicted the damage still moved through the young potato plants. There were two of them, flying French flags. They lumbered majestically through the field, their guns still trained right at us. I thought I could still see a wisp of smoke rising from each barrel, but they didn't fire anymore. They must have seen our waving handkerchiefs and understood.

This isn't real, I thought. It's like a stage set or something. Just two tanks in a sunny field. Is that our liberation?

My friend Sarah nudged me and I looked back. The Germans had hung a huge sheet out of a top-floor window of the main house. They were surrendering!

We ran back to the administration building and clustered around the main gate. The Germans were piling into the trucks and cars that stood packed and waiting for them in the courtyard. One of the guards opened the gate to the camp. Then he too jumped into a truck.

As the truck careened around the corner, we swarmed into the courtyard, up the steps to the terrace, around the corner to the front of the house. There was a war being waged at our doorstep, but where was the battle being fought?

Sarah was right beside me. "Look, isn't that Mr. Cunningham?" she whispered. Our tall, dignified English camp leader was striding purposefully across the courtyard, conferring with the German commandant. Together the two men got into the German staff car.

"He's going to look for the Allied army commander," somebody explained. "We are in a war zone. We need protection for the camp."

I stood with the rest of them — too excited to go inside, to do anything while we waited. My heart pounded, my pulse raced. This was it — the moment I had waited for!

I don't know how long we waited — hours, I guess. Long enough to worry whether Mr. Cunningham had found the Allied commander, whether the battle around Biberach was going well. I had found my parents in the crowd and we sat down together on the balustrade of the terrace, holding each other, waiting in silence.

Then a dusty jeep roared into the courtyard. Mr. Cunningham was back!

He jumped out of the jeep, followed by the driver, a young French sergeant in equally dusty battle fatigues. Together they went into the administration building. A moment later they appeared on a small balcony overlooking the camp compound.

Even at that distance I could see that Mr. Cunningham was smiling broadly. Next to his towering frame, the small French sergeant looked frail and unassuming. His khaki blouse was crumpled and his narrow face looked tired and drawn under his grimy helmet. He had come straight from the battlefield — a shy and embarrassed emissary from the Allied armies.

I didn't know I was shouting with the others until my throat felt dry and raw. But I went on croaking my cheers until the French sergeant raised both arms to signal for silence.

There was a hush. The soldier took off his helmet and looked down at our expectant faces.

He smiled self-consciously.

"T'ank you," he said in his heavy French accent. "T'ank you, t'ank you all very much." It was the limit of his English vocabulary. But nobody cared. After all, he was there. It was his presence that counted, not his words!

Everybody began to cheer and shout and applaud again. No, not everybody. Next to me a woman I knew was crying silently. Her husband had died during the first few days after we had left Belsen. To her this moment must seem bitter indeed. Her tears made me think of Grannie — and of everybody else who hadn't lived to experience this day. I swallowed hard. Then I pushed this pain away to the back of my mind. I wanted to be joyful. I could grieve later.

The French sergeant still stood on the balcony, accepting our cheers and applause with quiet dignity. Did he feel strange being showered like this with love and gratitude? I couldn't tell. Perhaps someday he would tell his grandchildren about this special moment right in the middle of a battle.

Then he was gone, back in his jeep, driving off toward the town. For him the battle was not over. The rest of the war still had to be won.

I stared after him, still under the spell of the moment. This little man with his self-conscious thank-yous had touched something deep in me. He is a symbol, I thought. He is Victory, the Liberator, Freedom, Peace — all rolled in one.

Peace! I suddenly laughed. To me peace will never be a dove with an olive branch, or an angel with golden wings. My symbol of peace wears a khaki shirt and a dusty helmet and army boots!

Chapter 20

WE WERE GOING to town! I'd thought the moment would never come. For five long days we had waited for the battle zone to move away from us. Day after day we still heard the sounds of heavy artillery in the distance. We couldn't actually see or feel the war, but the French army commander insisted that it wasn't safe for us to leave the camp. There were all kinds of rumors about "Werewolves"—fanatic Nazis said to be roaming the countryside in search of straggling Allied soldiers or liberated prisoners like us. I could imagine what they would do to us. No, for the moment I was glad for the gates and barbed wire. Our erstwhile prison had become a little fortress sheltering us within its walls. I kept looking up at the flagpole on top of the Big House where the British Union Jack now rippled in the breeze instead of the red, white, and black Nazi banner. It made me feel warm and happy and protected.

But now the war had finally moved so far away from Biberach that even the French commander felt that the gates of the camp could be opened. We were warned to go out in groups, to limit our excursions to daytime hours. But otherwise we were free to go anywhere in the immediate surroundings.

My mother and I set out in a group of five. There was Betty, a friend of ours from Belsen, and two English women who had become good friends more recently. Lois was a tall, thin, ex-schoolteacher with a wonderful dry sense of humor; Kay, a brisk, efficient, gray-haired woman had lived all over the world with her colonel husband until they had retired to the island of Guernsey shortly before the war. They were both wonderful company and we were in a gay and expectant mood as we set out on the twenty-minute downhill walk to town.

Not one of us had any idea what Biberach was like. The railroad station from which we had been brought to the camp lay on the outskirts of the town and we had arrived when it was dark. Gradually, as we approached the populated area, we became more silent and subdued. What kind of reception would we get from the defeated German population? They'd realize of course right away who we were. They just needed to take a look at our clothes and shoes. Would they be nasty and unfriendly? Or would they be afraid of us? Secretly I hoped that there would be lots of French soldiers about in the town to give us moral support.

We had come about halfway down the hill when Lois suddenly darted over to the side of the road and bent down to pick up something from the gutter. There was lots of debris scattered all over the place — left from the day before our liberation when all those hundreds of people had fled from Ulm along this road. What was it that Lois had spotted among all that litter?

She came running back to us, triumphantly waving a scrap of paper in her hand.

"Look what I found," she shouted. "I found money! Lots of it! We are rich!"

We clustered around her to examine her find. It was money all right — a large, faded bill, torn and dirty. But what made us all stare at each other in disbelief for a moment was its denomination. In clear bold letters across the bill it said: *Eine Million Mark*. One Million Marks!

My mother and Betty started to laugh simultaneously. Kay, who was still examining the bill earnestly, looked up startled. And Lois and I were puzzled too. We couldn't understand what was so funny.

Betty regained her composure first.

"Sorry to shatter your illusions," she said. "But that bill isn't worth the paper it's printed on. This is inflation money — the kind they printed by the bushel right after World War I when Germany went through that awful inflation. I wonder why the dickens anyone would have wanted to carry this along when they were fleeing from the bombings. Why anyone would still have it, to begin with."

"I guess we'll never know," Lois sighed, her face long with disappointment. "What a shame. I was already beginning to imagine all the things we could have bought with it."

She started to crumple the bill to toss it back into the gutter, but suddenly Kay snatched it out of her hand.

"Nonsense," she said. "This is money and it doesn't say anywhere that it is out of date. I'm going to town and I will buy things with this."

With a determined gesture, she smoothed out the bill and after folding it carefully, she tucked it into the pocket of her suit jacket.

All the rest of the way to town, my mother and Betty and Lois tried to convince Kay that the bill was no good. Kay was adamant. She was determined to go shopping. Secretly I sympathized with her. It was so awful not to have any money in your pocket. I too wanted very much to buy something in town.

Biberach turned out to be a charming medieval town with a good-sized cathedral and a lovely fountain on its main square. There were narrow cobblestoned streets lined with small shops and larger, more substantial stores around the main square. There was not much merchandise displayed in the windows because of all the war shortages, but to me, anything new seemed a miracle.

It felt odd, strolling around like that as if we were just a group of ordinary sightseers and window-shoppers. I felt the glances of the local people burning in my back as we passed, but there were quite a few French soldiers lounging about and that made us feel safe.

On the square, we stopped in front of a shoe store. It wasn't much of a window display. A dozen or so flat-heeled sandals, their soles made of some kind of composition material, the tops made of interlaced straps of multicolored imitation leather. They looked just wonderful to me. Imagine, a pair like that instead of the horrible beige pumps that I still loathed with a passion. It was enough to make my mouth water.

Kay noticed the longing in my eyes.

"Come on," she said. "Let's go in and buy Rosie a pair. Let's buy some for all of us."

My mother and Betty had long since given up trying to talk Kay out of using Lois' worthless money. Now we all trooped into the store — half amused, half worried about what would develop.

The store owner eyed us warily. He must have guessed who we were and I don't think he was anxious to serve us. But he had no choice. Since neither Kay nor Lois could speak German, my mother took the initiative and explained what we wanted to buy.

It turned out that the striped sandals were really the only kind of shoes the man had in his store. Soon all five of us had been fitted with a pair. I wriggled my toes blissfully. The light, open shoes felt wonderful on my feet.

Now came the moment to pay for our purchases. We looked at Kay. Grandly, Kay reached into her pocket and brought out the soiled one-million-mark bill. Quite casually she handed it to the salesman and stood as if waiting for her change.

The salesman stared at the bill. The expression on his face was quite interesting. His mouth dropped open a little and his eyes looked glazed. Worriedly, he marched over to the cash register and then he and the woman cashier had a short but agitated conference.

The salesman returned, shaking his head. He looked like a man whose suspicions had been confirmed. He explained the invalidity of the bill to us and indicated that we would either have to produce proper marks or else leave without the shoes. To underscore his words, he scooped up Kay's pair of sandals and started to put them back in the box. The rest of us already had our new shoes on our feet.

Kay started to protest — in English. The man countered with an insulting remark, which Kay happened to understand.

I think until that moment Kay, like the rest of us, was really ready to accept the fact that the money was worthless and prepared to leave the store without a purchase. We had done it for fun, to see what would happen — in a spirit of reckless excitement.

But the insult directed at her brought out Kay's fighting spirit.

With a defiant gesture, she snatched back the million-mark bill.

"We'll see whether this money is legal tender or not," she snapped. "You wait here and I'll go see the French commander. He will decide. And don't you dare take off those shoes in the meantime."

She swept out of the store. Through the plate-glass window we could watch her stride purposefully across the square to the former City Hall building where the French army had set up occupation headquarters.

The rest of us waited on our green leather chairs in uneasy silence. The store people glared at us, or perhaps at our feet, still so prominently garbed in unpaid merchandise. I suppose they were afraid to tell us to take them off. After all, the army people were bound to be on our side.

It wasn't a long wait. Within minutes Kay returned triumphantly across the square, a young French officer at her side.

The French commander had been most charming. He had received her graciously, had looked at the bill and agreed at once that the store should accept it at its face value. The young officer had come along to see that this decision was enforced. Obviously the French commander had never heard about German inflation money either.

Now the store owner became frantic. Realizing that my mother was the only one who could understand him, he turned to her and began to pour out his woes in a rapid volley of words. We couldn't be serious, could we, to expect change of 999,978 marks? He could never raise that amount of money — his whole store wasn't worth a fraction of that amount.

My mother looked at Kay, but she shook her

head. Once again the officer pointed at the un-happy man and said in broken German: "You pay. You give change."

I squirmed on my chair, uncomfortable. The thing had gone too far! It had been a joke, a prank — but now it had turned into something more. The store owner had sunk into one of his green leather chairs, his face ashen. The cashier, who seemed to be his wife, was sobbing loudly.

"Please," she pleaded. "Please take your shoes. Take all our shoes. But don't insist on the change!"

Once again my mother turned to Kay. "Don't you think that would be enough?" she asked. "I'm getting sorry for these people."

Kay looked at her scornfully.

"I'm surprised at you," she said. "Getting all soft and tenderhearted. You — after all you've been through. Don't you hate the bastards? I do!"

"Hate?" my mother said softly. "I really don't want to hate. It's such a futile emotion. It tears you all up inside — and for what? Do you think any of them will care if we hate them? They'll just laugh at us. Hating hurts no one but your-self!"

Kay looked at each of us in turn. Then she threw up her hands in a gesture of defeat.

"Oh, all right," she said. "You're all just a bunch of softies. Do you think this staunch fellow over there worried about us all the years we were sitting in that camp up on the hill? He most likely never gave us a thought!"

She scooped up her shoebox and she flounced

out of the store without looking back once at the owner. The rest of us followed carrying our own old shoes. The store people flocked after us, babbling their gratitude and relief.

Outside Kay thanked the French officer for his assistance. Then we walked silently through the town on our way back to the camp. I walked behind the others, my thoughts in turmoil. I was all mixed up about what I wanted to feel.

Like Kay, I wanted to hate — to get even, to get revenge for all the things that had happened to me. But instead I only felt sorry for the shoe store man, just like my mother. What was wrong with me? What was wrong with both of us?

I summoned up the face of the little shoe store owner and in my mind I tried to direct hate at him. But it was no good. He seemed like such a pathetic fellow, I didn't even feel particularly good about having made him squirm a bit. In fact, I felt a little guilty that we had made him give us five pairs of his shoes. I tried to think of Red Müller, and Lübke, and all the Gestapo officers I had hated over the years. But that didn't work either. I just couldn't hate the shoe store owner in their stead.

My mother was right, I thought. It takes too much effort to hate. It is too painful. I don't want to be angry and bitter and all cold and hard inside. The day is too nice, and the sun is shining and I am walking with lovely new shoes. I am free at last!

Chapter 21

IT WASN'T ALWAYS easy to be free. Now there were new problems to consider — the problems of the future. Freedom meant going back into a normal world, living a normal life. For my father it meant thoughts of how he would earn a living. For me it meant wondering what I would do with my life. Go back to school? I was seventeen. Back in Amsterdam, Anneke would be graduating from the Lyceum this summer. And I had finished only one makeshift high school year. How could I go back? Could one ever go back?

Freedom also brought knowledge of things we didn't really want to know. The truth about what really had happened in Poland. Bit of news and stories trickled in. About Auschwitz, the death camp. Was it really true? Was that what happened? The old and the sick, the small children and their mothers — sent to the gas chambers right from the trains? So that was what the French women in the Belsen tent camp had meant when they yelled across the fences: *"Ils ont brulées nos enfants* [they have burned our children]." How naïve we had been! We had thought they were talking about a barracks fire.

I tried to picture the arrival scenes in Auschwitz — the people tumbling out of those ghastly trains, then having to strip naked on the snowy platform for a life and death selection: those who could work to the right, the others to the left, to line up before the gas chambers.

No, I couldn't bear to picture it. The people I saw in my mind's eye had faces, faces I knew. And the children — the little children who had been sent alone — who didn't even have a mother's loving arms around them to ease the death agony as they choked and gasped out their lives, herded together in that "shower" chamber.

So it had all been a lie! All the talk about labor camps and "resettlement in the east." A carefully nurtured lie to make people compliant, to keep them from fighting back. Always the hope that if you do what you're told, you'll survive somehow . . . survive and live to see the liberation. Because you knew what happened if you didn't do what you were told. That meant death right away, possibly torture. Well, in the end obedience too had brought death.

And I? How had I escaped? And why? Was it chance? Was it coincidence? Or was it God?

Or was it my mother, who had struggled so

hard to make us survive? Was it being with my parents that had given me the strength to live?

In a rush of affection I thought of my parents, both so different and yet both strong in their own ways. Step by step they had been with me, had helped me through the horrible years. My mother, growing stronger, more practical, and more active with each succeeding crisis. And my father, with his calm detachment and his secret inner smile, letting the events sweep around him and carry him along without permitting them to disturb his innermost balance. Both of them had infuriated me at times, but I had drawn strength of different kinds from each.

Then I thought of Grannie. What had my father said when we learned of her death in Belsen? "At least we know how she died." She had died on a bed, a natural death. God *had* been merciful.

And we were here — free from the fences, but still not free to leave, to go home.

Home? What was home? An empty shell of a house? A house without any of the things we had treasured?

Freedom brought new words, a new vocabulary. "Repatriation" was one new word. The British in the camp went first. Planes came to take them home. We embraced, we said goodbye, we sent letters along for relatives abroad, we exchanged addresses. The planes flew in formation over the camp and we stood in the courtyard and waved and waved.

The man from Holland came. My heart beat

faster. Now it was our turn. Now we would go home to Holland!

The man looked at our papers. "Only Dutch citizens," he said. "You are stateless. We can repatriate only our own citizens now."

We stared at him, not comprehending.

"But we were residents of Holland," my father said. "Our house is there, my business, we were deported from Holland."

"Sorry," said the man. "Only Dutch citizens."

When the planes flying to Holland passed over the camp, I didn't look up and I didn't wave. I stayed inside the barracks and I closed my ears to the drone of the airplane engines.

What was left? Our South American passports? Scraps of paper that had saved our lives. Thank you, Paraguay, for helping us survive. We couldn't really expect more from these passports. Now they were just bits of paper, their usefulness at an end.

"Displaced Persons" was another new phrase. Such a small handful of us left now in the camp that once had held almost two thousand.

Sarah and her family were left behind too.

"We'll be going to Palestine," Sarah said. "As soon as we can apply for entry permits. Won't it be wonderful to see Jerusalem at last!"

I stared at Sarah. Palestine? It was a word out of the past. How long was it since I had thought of Zionism?

"If you want to go to Palestine we won't stand in your way, Rosemarie," my father said. "You are nearly grown up. You must make your own decisions."

But the decision was not that easy. How lucky Sarah was to have no doubts. I wished I too could have her single-minded sense of purpose, her clear, unwavering faith in Zionism as a way of life.

I went for a walk. Out of the camp, up the path between the wheat fields to the little hill topped by a beech tree and a bench. From that bench you could survey the surrounding countryside for miles. In the shade of that beech tree you could think and be alone.

Alone! "In the long run we are all alone." Grannie had said that, a long time ago. And it was true. I had been alone. In the midst of a crowded barracks — in a flash of intuition — I had known that she was right.

If not Palestine, then what? Holland had disowned me. To Austria, there was no returning. America then — America, where our relatives had gone. I tried to remember what I had learned about the United States. In America, all kinds of people had learned to live together. Perhaps in America I might blend in — feel that I belonged.

A long time ago I had stood before my bathroom mirror and had wondered who and what I was. And now, years later, the question still remained. Who was I? Where did I belong? Rosemarie Brenner — Stateless — who didn't belong anywhere.

I looked out across the fields below me where the farmers were busy gathering the hay. With their pitchforks they were scooping the hay into symmetrical hillocks, moving rhythmically under the hot sun.

Before me a butterfly fluttered in the field. I looked at the butterfly. White, gossamer wings, hovering over a yellow buttercup . . . over a daisy . . . resting briefly on a swaying stalk of green grass.

You and I, little butterfly, new to this world, fresh out of our cocoons, our wings still wet. Like you, little butterfly, I am new, a new me, a new life before me.

I sat still, thoughts tumbling around in my head.

"I Am That I Am." Who had said that? God had said it to Moses on a mountaintop. I Am That I Am. I am I. I am Rosemarie.

Suddenly it didn't matter that I didn't have a state or a home at the moment. It didn't matter that I didn't know what kind of life lay before me.

I jumped up. "I am Rosemarie," I shouted at the butterfly. My voice was so strong that it carried over the fields and the farmers, hearing it, looked up curiously.

But I didn't care. I was free — really free now — free to be and feel myself.

I started to run down the hill, through the fields, toward the camp. I felt the wind in my face and my hair was almost long enough again to blow behind me in the breeze.

Author's Note

DURING WORLD WAR II, when Hitler's German army occupied a large part of Europe, Hitler ordered the destruction of Europe's Jews. It was what he called his "Final Solution" to the "Jewish Problem."

It is said that Hitler was insane and that his persecution of the Jews was one symptom of a diseased mind. The amazing thing about the whole "holocaust" era is that he found so many willing helpers among the German population to execute his paranoid scheme!

From all of the occupied countries Jews were sent to the Polish extermination camps. The true nature of these camps was carefully disguised. The secret was so well kept that most of the victims didn't learn of their true fate until they waited in line to be killed in the gas chambers.

By the end of the war more than six million men, women, and children had gone to their deaths in these infamous camps. Very few survived. Hitler's henchmen were incredibly efficient and thorough in their quest. While the German army lost the war against the Allies, the Gestapo won the war against the Jews.

Rosemarie Brenner, the girl in this story, is one survivor of the holocaust. She survived through a combination of chance, luck, coincidence — and a strong desire to live. In this sense her story is not typical, for to survive was not typical at all. But as she proceeded on her journey to survival, she experienced many of the things experienced by the countless thousands who did not survive.

Like all the characters in this story, Rosemarie is an invention of the author — a composite — based on very real people who lived through all the things described in this book. All the events in this story — the places, backgrounds, and circumstances — are absolutely true. The camps are real and everything that happened there, down to the names of the SS guards.

To all those who did not live to tell about their sufferings this book is dedicated. They should not be forgotten. Are we sure that nothing like this will ever happen to anyone again?